Over and Back

S.E. Martin

Apostrophe H

For my husband, who believes in me even when I hesitate to believe in myself. Nia:wen for always being my biggest supporter.

Chapter 1

Ganĕhdo'k'ah
The end of the leaves

Zeke

I've had a lacrosse stick in my hands since I was born.

My first stick was tiny, less than a foot in length, with a hickory shaft and colorful cord threading the curved head. It was handmade by a traditional stickmaker from a nearby reservation. Haudenosaunee men, like me, are often buried with these original wooden sticks as they begin their journeys home to the Creator.

As a professional player, my current stick is made of metal and plastic. It's lightweight for making quick shots on net, but durable enough to withstand heavy checks from defenders. My stick is an extension of my body, enabling me to play the game of my ancestors at the highest level. Lacrosse has always been foundational to my happy memories and family gatherings.

I think back to one of the many times my grandparents came over for dinner when I was around ten years old. My mother shooed her four young sons outside to play so she and my grandmother could finish cooking. It was a warm day in June, and the delectable scents of corn soup and hamburgers wafted from the house.

"Grandpa! Grandpa! Come watch us!" my brother Miles pleaded eagerly, his lacrosse stick in hand.

My grandfather chuckled as Miles and Ezra, my youngest brother, tugged on his shirt to pull him outside. "Do you need a referee?"

"That's my job," my dad said with a smile, following us outside, "but these wild wolves could use your coaching wisdom." His kind eyes sparkled as he pulled over a plastic chair for his father.

It was always special to play lacrosse in the backyard with my dad and grandfather. They gave us so much of their time and attention, teaching us the game and guiding us to be good teammates. Backyard ball was the best. We could be creative with our shots and try new approaches without fear of making mistakes.

I fought for a loose ball with Jordan, the brother closest to me in age, our sticks clattering loudly together as we tried to push each other out of the way. Our dingy sneakers kicked the earth, trying to untangle the ball between our feet.

"Boys, be careful of–" my father called out.

Jordan scooped the ball with his stick and spun in the opposite direction, not seeing four year old Ezra until it was too late.

Ezra went crashing to the ground and began to wail.

I dropped my stick and rushed over to him, kneeling to check him for injuries.

Jordan hung back, likely afraid he was about to get in trouble for knocking our baby brother over.

"You OK, Ezzie?" I asked.

Ezra threw himself into my arms, tears running down his little cheeks.

I hugged him as my dad jogged over, grabbing my stick on his way.

"Thanks for checking on your brother, Zeke," my dad said gratefully. "Just remember to never throw your stick on the ground." He handed it back to me. "I know you wanted to get to Ezra quickly, but you have to respect your stick."

I took it from him, wincing at my mistake. "Sorry, Dad. I wasn't thinking."

"It's OK." He ruffled my dark hair as he planted a kiss on Ezra's head. "It can be easy to forget, but it's important." He smiled warmly over at Jordan, reassuring him.

"Our people are the guardians of *Dewá'ä:ö'*," my grandfather added, coming over to lift Ezra into his arms. "You're honoring the Creator when you play our game of lacrosse. We treat our sticks well because then they will do the same for us."

I nodded, taking my responsibility seriously then, as I do now.

The *thump* of equipment being tossed into a nearby stall pulls me from my memories. I smile, reaching for my helmet as I tune back into the sights and sounds of the Buffalo Outlaws locker room. Players are chatting amiably as they dress for practice, velcro ripping as they adjust arm guards and rib protectors before pulling on jerseys. It's the first day of training camp with my new team, and I'm feeling reflective. The Outlaws are the hometown team I grew up cheering for with my family. My dad never missed watching a game.

He would have loved seeing me as an Outlaw.

"You're all smiles today," my friend and team captain, Jamie Montour, says.

We walk out of the locker room together, heading for the arena floor.

"It's good to be home," I reply, taking in the familiar orange and black team logo at midfield.

"Well, we're glad to have you." He grins. "I wish you would've signed in Buffalo years ago."

I shrug. "I'm loyal. I wanted to stay with the team that drafted me. I don't think I would have left if I hadn't been traded."

"You're welcome, by the way." Jamie elbows me. "I've been pleading with Coach to get you here since we played together at Nationals last year. It's been a pain in the ass playing against you while you were with Vegas."

I chuckle and scoop up a ball nearby, spinning and cradling it in my stick as we talk. "Try playing against *you*. You're a menace."

He grins wolfishly. "That's because I'm a trash talker."

"It has nothing to do with being a future Hall of Famer, I'm sure," I quip, turning my body to whip the ball into an empty net. Jamie's a generational talent from Six Nations reserve in Ontario. Every lacrosse player knows who Jamie Montour is, not just the Indigenous ones.

Coach Travis blows his whistle, calling the team together to strategize for the day.

Three hours later we're gassed. Morning practice is drawing to a close, and I'm ready for some food and a nap before facing the second half of the day.

"Heads up, Z!" Jamie hollers at me as he launches a pass. I catch the ball and it lands with a satisfying *plop* in my stick's mesh. A rookie defenseman is covering me, and I feel momentarily guilty before faking him out to the left and then rolling to my right. I turn on the jets, charging for the goal and leaving him in my dust. Another defender is coming towards me, so I set my position and shoot, my stick starting low on my body before rising higher as I release the ball. It sails past the goaltender's shoulder and into the net.

I pump my fist in celebration as my teammates come by to congratulate me. It's only practice, but it always feels good to score.

"Nice shot, man." Sawyer Lane jogs over to bump his glove against mine, grinning widely. "I'm glad you won't be scoring those *against* us anymore."

"I've got to keep up with you," I say. "What were you, top ten in league goals last year?"

He holds up his stretched-out palm. "Number five, baby! On my way to number one."

"Careful, Lanes. If your head gets any bigger you're going to need a new bucket." Jamie bops him on the helmet as he walks by.

"I'm like a tropical bird during mating season," Sawyer preens. "The bigger my head gets, the better my luck."

"Keep telling yourself that." Jamie calls over his shoulder. He finds the rookie defenseman I'd beaten on the last play, giving him a gentle stick tap. "Keep your head up, Wes. Zeke's a master at rushing the net. You'll learn a lot from practicing against him."

"Damn, man." Wes Harrison bends over, hands on his thighs as he gulps in a few deep breaths. "That was a hell of a spin move you put on me."

I chuckle and clap him on the shoulder. "Sorry about that."

A shrill whistle grabs our attention. It's time to break down our final plays.

I peel off my sweaty equipment once we're back in the locker room, my legs heavy from exertion. Wes sits in the stall next to mine, gingerly kicking off his sneakers.

"The first day of camp is always brutal," I reassure him with a smile. "I keep in shape during the off-season, but I'm still worn out once we're back to practice."

He groans. "This is going to be different from college ball. I'm not used to getting my ass handed to me every play."

I laugh. "You'll adjust. You belong in the pros. You wouldn't have been drafted if you didn't."

He pulls his jersey over his head and chucks it into the nearby laundry bin. "I feel like a fish out of water. I'm missing

Wisconsin and my Oneida family. I'm getting beat up on the floor." He blows out a frustrated breath.

My heart goes out to him. Rookie year is tough, let alone also leaving your home and your people.

"I'm feeling out of my element right now, too," I commiserate. "I'm moving back home since I'm not playing on the west coast anymore. I'm happy about it, but –"

I pause, my first instinct to clam up. Vulnerability is not my strong suit. I pull in a deep breath and force myself to continue. "My family and friends have been through hard times. I'm not sure what to expect."

I'm thinking, of course, of my dad. But also of Genesee Skye.

My heart always comes back to Genny whenever I let my guard down. She was my best friend and first love. My only love, really. That was until my life fell apart, and our friendship with it. We haven't talked since I was in college.

"That makes two of us," Wes nods grimly. "But I'm not discouraged. I'm going to work my ass off these next four weeks to make the starting roster."

I like this kid.

"You need a training buddy? I'm looking for one," I ask, seeing the opportunity to mentor a young Indigenous player.

Wes brightens. "I'd love that. Where do you live?"

I strip off the remainder of my gear. "I'm on the Cattaraugus rez. You?"

"I'm not far from there, so I can come to you," he offers. "I'd love to check out your community."

"Yeah, man. Come on over." I grab a towel. "The Haudenosaunee are one big family of six nations."

He grins. "You sure the Senecas won't kick me out?"

I smile widely. "I'll tell the Tribal Marshals to stand down."

The hot water is soothing to my sore muscles once I hit the showers. I bow my head in the powerful stream, letting the water soak my hair and run down my face. Dread coils in my stomach as I consider my upcoming move back home. I feel a nagging unease about facing the aftermath of the tragedy that rocked my world ten years ago.

I push down the discomfort and roughly comb my hair out of my eyes. The trade to Buffalo is a fresh start, and I plan to make the most of it.

Chapter 2

Gahsá'kneh
November

Genny

I smile before I even open my eyes. Crisp fall air breezes across my skin, wafting the scent of morning dew on fallen leaves into my bedroom.

It's November 1.

November is the moody girl of the autumn months with her gray days and leafless trees. As a fellow moody girl, I dress like November shows up – in an array of dark colors and sensible footwear.

The landscape is stark as Mother Earth begins her slow descent into winter rest. Soon we'll preserve food from the fall harvest, carve out icy tracks for Snow Snake tournaments, and eventually tap maple trees as spring approaches. Each year I look forward to the coziness of home and community during these cold months.

Yesterday, on Halloween, I stayed nestled under my comforter until my alarm insisted I get up. Today I leap out of bed, throwing my legs over the side and bouncing up to get dressed. I'm giddy with joy that my favorite month of the year is here. Morning runs are the best when temperatures are brisk, my sneakers crunching leaves underfoot as I dodge acorns. I'll throw on a big, cozy cardigan afterwards, stepping outside to drink coffee and warm up on the porch.

I hum happily as I pull on my running clothes, eager to head outside. There's a distinctly November coldness in the air today, and I'm jazzed. My headphones are over my ears and pumping out a high-energy playlist before I'm even out the front door.

My breath comes out in icy puffs as I keep a steady pace around the neighborhood. I smile and wave at a young mother buckling her fussy infant into a stroller. She bears the dark circles of an interrupted night of sleep.

"You're doing great," I say to her as I come to a stop.

The baby stops crying to look at me, startled by my appearance. I waggle my fingers at him and he smiles.

"It doesn't feel like it, but I'm trying," she responds with a sigh. "Our morning walk usually settles us both down."

I smile. "I love my daily routines, too. I crave them when life interferes."

We chat for a few minutes before the baby starts to whine. We part and I continue on my path.

I'm a traditional girl, and I long for a family and children of my own. I thought I knew who I wanted to grow old beside, but that dream ended long ago. Dating is a drag. I know every man on the Cattaraugus reservation, and they all bore me. I want to marry someone from my culture, but damn, the prospects are depressing.

I round the corner towards my house, slowing to a walk and catching my breath. I haven't lost hope in finding my dream romantic partner, but at twenty-seven I have much less patience (and time) for men who still want to act like boys.

I pull open the front door and head to the kitchen, intent on starting the coffee pot for my beloved post-run cup of coffee. I open the cabinet next to the fridge and my heart sinks. In the busyness of life, I'd forgotten to stop at the store yesterday. I was out of a crucial ingredient for my perfect November morning: coffee grounds.

I tap my forehead against the cabinet door in frustration. Dammit.

I drift back towards my room with a pained sigh. I can leave early and grab a coffee to-go on my drive into school. It's not the idyllic morning I'd planned, but it would do. I tug open the front door as I walk by, wanting to bring even more crisp fall air inside the house.

I jump back with a small screech as I find my older sister and roommate, Mackenzie, climbing the top step, two distinctive red cups in her hands. She raises her eyes in concern at my shriek, then starts to laugh.

"Is this the thanks I get for picking up Pumpkin Spice Lattes from Tim's?"

"You scared the daylights out of me!" I gulp in a few breaths and lean against the door. One hand clutches my pounding heart and the other eagerly reaches for the warm beverage from our nearby Tim Horton's coffee shop.

My 5th grade classroom is buzzing at the first bell. I've been hyping them up for November 1, as well. It marks the start of Native American Heritage Month, and the school celebrates it enthusiastically. Many of our students and teachers are from the Seneca Nation, and it's an occasion to infuse our lessons with the beauty of our culture.

I project a map of New York State onto the whiteboard as my students settle into their seats.

"Let's talk about the Haudenosaunee people," I say. "You probably already know a lot about them because we live in their homelands. How many tribal nations make up the Haudenosaunee Confederacy?"

A girl in front eagerly raises her hand. "Six!"

I grin. "Six, very good! What are some of those nations? You can call them out."

Voices burst across the room like popcorn.

"Seneca!" A boy from Cattaraugus shouts.

"Like us," I say, smiling at him.

"Tuscarora!" A girl whose dad is Tuscarora pipes up.

I label the map as the names roll in, showing where each tribe has reservations. "Keep it coming."

"Onondaga! Like those brothers that play lacrosse." One of the non-Native kids volunteers.

"Mohawk? Is that one?" a student asks hesitantly.

"Yep. There's a Mohawk community up here," I circle an area on the map, "and also several communities in Canada." I indicate regions in Ontario and Quebec.

We add the Cayugas and the Oneidas to the map, as well. We discuss how the six Haudenosaunee nations work well together because they have a shared culture and history.

My heart soars later in the day as I walk around the classroom. Students are paired up and making plans to build traditional longhouse dioramas for our unit projects. They're chattering happily as I stop to check on each group. I love my job.

What I *don't* love is fighting with the printer after school. Mackenzie walks into the breakroom at 4:30pm to find me swearing and sweating. The machine had jammed while I was making copies of tomorrow's worksheets, and was still insisting there was paper trapped inside. I'm taking it apart for a third time when my sister waves to get my attention.

"Ready to go home? The office is closed so I'm done." She taps her foot and looks at me with impatience.

"This thing won't print," I huff, slamming shut the front panel.

"Let me look at it. I'm a printer whisperer." She walks over and eyes the screen.

I collapse with a sigh at the table nearby. I'm so ready to be done with my day. After this, I'm helping with a craft event at the library. Then I'm bringing meals to elders who recently had surgery. I'll have to forage for dinner leftovers before heading to bed and doing it all again tomorrow.

"Hey, so," Mackenzie begins, opening the back panel of the printer, "Linda Jimerson in the office told me that her son's helping with a construction project at the Jacobs' house." She eyes me warily before pulling out the tiniest scrap of paper I've ever seen from between the rollers. "Ah ha! Found the problem."

"You have got to be kidding me," I groan. "That's all it was?"

"I told you, I'm a printer whisperer." She shuts the back panel and the machine hums happily to life. "Anyway, Linda says Elaine is adding an apartment above the garage."

Elaine Jacobs is our mom's best friend, and our families have grown up together. I've helped her out for years, ever since her husband, David, passed away during my senior year of high school. I'm regularly at her house.

"That's nice. I noticed construction out back, but hadn't asked about it." I get to my feet and retrieve my copies, which are finally being spit out into the printer tray.

Mackenzie clears her throat. "Yeah. It's, uh–"

I look up at her, sensing something unpleasant. "It's what?"

She smiles tightly. "It's for Zeke. He's moving back home."

I freeze, papers hitting my hands as they continue coming out of the printer.

"He got traded to the Outlaws over the summer," she explains.

"I knew that. But he already lived in downtown Buffalo."

She shrugs. "I guess he wants to spend more time with his family now that he won't be traveling to Vegas."

I stare blankly at my copies, now laying still in a pile. "Dammit."

My sister squeezes my shoulder. "We'll figure it out, I promise. Now, let's get out of here."

We drive home in silence. Mackenzie scrolls on her phone while my mind turns over this latest development.

Zeke Jacobs had been the love of my life, and he'd broken my heart. If he was moving back to Cattaraugus, then I was in serious trouble.

We had been inseparable since toddlerhood. Falling for him was like slipping on a cozy sweater in November. After years of false starts, he finally asked me to our senior prom. I planned to tell him how I felt that night and kiss him on the dancefloor. It sounded terribly romantic to seventeen year old Genny and her friends.

But then everything changed. I went from being the center of his world to getting ghosted. His eyes had always looked at me with mirth and adoration. Now, they were empty and dull in my presence.

Zeke has been a bottomless well of grief for me ever since. Whenever I have a bad date I curse his existence, angry at him for ruining what was supposed to be our future together. I was stuck dating losers because, in my mind, Zeke and I were supposed to end up together.

I don't know what's next for us. We'd barely interacted in years, even though I was still involved with his family. I don't want to spend the rest of my life hating him, but I dread the thought of spending time with him.

I exhale forcefully, blowing away some rogue hairs that had escaped my braid.

Mackenzie glances over. "You OK?"

"Just peachy," I reply in a sing-song tone. "Just thinking of everything I need to do tonight."

"Mmm hmm." She cocks an eyebrow in my direction. "Did you want to talk about it?"

My fingers clench around the steering wheel. I debate playing dumb with my sister, but decide against it. "No, not really."

She shrugs. "Suit yourself. But I think it would help."

I bite the inside of my cheek and ignore the weight in my chest as we approach our house.

Chapter 3

Zeke

B oom!

The mattress drops into place on the solid wood bed frame in my room.

I exhale with relief and high five my brother Jordan. We've been muscling the heavy pieces for an hour, sweating and swearing as my family pitched in to help set up my new apartment.

Jordan groans and flops onto the bed. "That was brutal, bro. I thought it would be easy moving that monstrosity from Mom's house."

"Yeah. It looked simple until we tried to lift it." I sit on the edge of the mattress, breathing heavily. "Beer for your efforts?"

"Hell yeah."

I leave Jordan scrolling on his phone and navigate through stacks of my belongings. I'm pulling an icy Labatt Blue from the fridge when my front door crashes open. Miles backs in with his arms full of cardboard boxes.

"More?" I groan, setting down the beer bottle and rushing to grab a container off the top.

He grunts and sets the rest on the kitchen table. "Mom claims these are the last ones. They look old." He blows off a layer of dust and promptly coughs.

I peek under one of the lids and see my high school graduation cap. His assessment is right on the money. They're boxes full of crap that only moms save.

"You got one of those Labatts for me?" Miles asks, making eyes at the beer I'd abandoned on the kitchen counter.

"Only if you bring one to Jordan while you're at it," I tease, sitting down at the table and opening one of the boxes. I might as well look through it before meeting Wes at the Community Center to train.

Miles grabs two bottles. "On it." He thumps my shoulder while heading to the bedroom. I smile when my brothers' laughter rings out. Watching dumb videos, no doubt.

I attack the mound of high school mementos: Graduation programs; newspaper clippings from football and lacrosse games; college admission letters. A few photos slide out from the pile. I flip through the photos and see a montage of high school life; me and my friends in the woods near the creek, playing lacrosse, screwing around in various cars.

My heart leaps when I see Genny.

Our mothers are best friends, so our two families grew up together. We spent nearly every day with each other. I played multiple sports, and she was one of the few people who could keep up with me. She was a star on our high school's lacrosse team. Countless days came to a close walking her home at twilight, my face hurting from smiling. I was crazy about her.

I grip a photo of us. We're on our backs in a lacrosse field. Genny's eyes are closed and crinkled from laughter. I'm beaming at her like a dumb fool in love. Because I was. I'd asked her to prom a week later. It was a leap of faith that paid off when she accepted my invitation.

A loud clatter startles me. The photo in my hand skitters across the table.

"Shit, you two," I swear. "You scared me."

Jordan chuckles after tossing his bottle into the recycling bin. "Whaddya got there?" he asks, glancing at the pictures spread before me.

"Just old junk from Mom," I mumble as I stand up. I drink half of a glass of water before I realize it's far too quiet. I turn to find the two of them exchanging glances. "What?"

Miles looks at Jordan, who narrows his eyes and sighs deeply.

I furrow my brow. "What's going on?"

"Nothing," Jordan responds shortly, still looking at Miles.

Miles swears under his breath and leans against the countertop, crossing his arms over his chest as he attempts to look nonchalant. "So. Looking at pictures of Genny?"

I stifle a groan and set my glass down loudly. "I told you, it's just clutter from Mom."

Jordan props his hip against the fridge. "She still lives on the rez, you know."

My eye twitches.

"We see her pretty often," he continues.

Miles coughs. I have officially had enough of whatever is up between these two.

"That's nice," I deadpan.

Jordan looks at me expectantly.

I stare back.

"You should call her sometime," Miles cuts in.

"I haven't talked to her in years," I huff impatiently.

"We know," they reply in unison.

I roll my eyes, hoping they leave soon.

Jordan drifts closer to the table and picks up a photo. "Don't you think it's time to put all this behind you?" he asks tentatively.

I dig in my fridge for a Gatorade. "All *what*?" I snap.

"Ignoring Genny," he responds quietly. "Pretending like losing Dad didn't fuck you up and you pushed her away."

I slam the refrigerator door shut. "I think we're done here."

Jordan's jaw ticks.

Miles clears his throat.

I close my eyes and breathe in deeply. I'm out of line and I know it.

"I'm sorry. I know you're trying to help," I say. "I appreciate all your time today."

"Anytime." Miles pulls me in for a quick hug. "We're really happy you're back home."

Jordan eyes me warily but joins the family embrace. "Don't worry about it, man. We're always here for you."

What was that about? I wonder a few minutes later. My family hardly ever mentions Genny. I run into her once or twice a year and that's it. It's better this way. I'd spent years hoping one day she'd love me as more than a friend. The way that I loved her. I never revealed my feelings and I'm glad. She's better off without me.

A long dormant memory nags at me as I change clothes. It was mid-May, and high school graduation was approaching. The sun was out, and the grass was freshly-cut. Genny and I were playing lacrosse at the community fields. Her rich brown locks were loosely braided, with wisps falling around her face as we battled for a loose ball.

"No." Our shoes bumped against each other as we kicked the ground. "Freaking." Sticks rattled as they collided. "Way." She planted her feet and unsuccessfully attempted to knock me off my position.

I smiled as we wrestled. "I'm winning this bet," I said.

"No, you're not," she responded, finally swiping the ball free from beneath us. She charged after it and I followed. I cut in front of her so I could block her path to the net.

I slashed my stick against hers, trying to dislodge the ball. She had it well protected in her pocket.

She was so beautiful. It was a problem every time I played against her, because she distracted me. She was wearing a navy blue East Lake High School tshirt and a pair of gray shorts. Her toffee skin was flushed from running around in the late spring warmth. I longed to hold her close and slowly unravel her silky hair with my hands.

Genny dodged me and I swore. This girl flustered me on an hourly basis.

I made a last ditch effort to foil her, extending my stick as I threw myself towards her.

She tried to avoid me but her feet caught on the shaft, sending her falling to the ground just shy of the net.

I started to whoop in celebration but, as usual, she was one step ahead of me. She flicked her stick as she fell, sending a weak bounce shot towards the goal. I scrambled but it was too late. The ball dribbled past the line, giving her the winning goal.

She rolled onto her back and raised her arms in the air, her laughter echoing across the open field.

I flopped onto the ground next to her. "Damn. Good game."

She looked over at me with a grin. "Pay up, loser."

I chuckled. "Fair is fair. What do you want with your one wish?"

She turned her gaze to the sky. The setting sun was painting it with blazing streaks of pink and orange. "Hmmm. What do I want?" She drummed her fingers against her chin as she thought.

I watched her with naked adoration. Our personalities and temperaments blended so well. It was as though I started where Genny ended, and vice versa. We were both headed to college in a few months, and my heart ached at the thought of being separated from her for the first time.

"How about...you buy me ice cream on the way home?"

I smiled. "That's easy. You got it."

She sat up, holding her stick in her lap. "Your turn."

I tilted my head in confusion. "What do you mean? I lost."

She looked down, tracing her finger along the soft blades of grass. "Yeah, but I want to know what you would've asked for if you'd won."

My heart started to pound. I knew exactly what I would've asked her.

"Come on." Genny gave me a gentle shove on the shoulder. "Tell me."

My mouth was suddenly dry. "Uh –"

She looked at me expectantly.

I scratched the back of my head, stalling for time.

Her fingers crawled to my other hand. She brushed the tips softly across my knuckles. "If you could have anything in the world right now, what would it be?" she asked.

Thump. Thump. The pounding in my chest intensified. I wanted to kiss her, but I wouldn't.

"I, uh –"

Her gaze was latched onto mine. She caught her lower lip between her teeth and my stomach clenched.

Here goes nothing.

"I would ask you – would you want – " My voice shook. "Go to prom with me."

Her eyes widened.

I panicked.

"I mean – if you want to, that is." I stumbled over my words. "*Do* you want to? It was supposed to be a question, not a demand." I felt my cheeks reddening.

In an instant she was in my arms, wrapping herself around my neck. I braced a forearm on the ground so we didn't topple over.

"Yes. I would love to go to prom with you." Genny pulled back and looked at me. Her face was lit up like a fireworks display.

It was my turn to grin. "Really?" I hesitantly snaked an arm around her waist.

She nodded enthusiastically. "Yes. Absolutely." Something flashed across her eyes and she breathed in deeply.

My stomach flipped as she leaned into me and dusted her lips across my cheek. My hand clenched on her hip. "Gen," I rasped.

"Yeah?" she asked softly.

I swallowed. Her lips were right there, and I burned with the desire to taste them. I bit the inside of my cheek to snap out of it.

"I'm really glad you'll go with me." I smiled and rose to my feet. My head was swimming and my body hummed with happiness. I offered her my hand and helped her up.

She wove her fingers between mine and squeezed. She kept her hand in mine until we reached the corner store. I bought her an ice cream bar and walked her back home as dusk settled around us.

Dammit. I run my hand through my hair, trying to shove the memory away. I've compartmentalized Genny in the dark recesses of my mind, not unlike the worn boxes hiding in my mom's closet.

I glance down at the photo of us on the table and my chest aches. I hadn't allowed that particular memory outside in years, and it hurt.

Because my dad died the night before prom. And then there was just...nothing. I had nothing left to give anyone besides my family. My life's path was disrupted by my dad's sudden death.

I grab my keys and head to my car. Wes and I are meeting up soon to practice, but my brain feels scrambled. A quick run beforehand would feel good and help me clear my head.

Chapter 4

Genny

My sneakers pound the trail beneath my feet, sending pebbles and twigs scattering. My rapid pace matches the angsty playlist in my ears. My high ponytail bounces with each stride. I breathe in deeply, inhaling the familiar, muddy scent of nearby Cattaraugus Creek. The surrounding trees and shrubs are brown and bare.

Physical activity is my stress relief. It's been a habit since childhood and my years as a high school athlete. Running, in particular, helps me unwind and balance my many responsibilities. I especially need it today to release some very specific anger and frustration.

Learning that Zeke was moving back home had thrown me for a loop. He'd lived in Buffalo the past five years while playing for Las Vegas on the weekends. I assumed he'd stay there after his trade to the Outlaws. Now that he'd be living on the rez and around more often, it was going to be difficult to avoid him. It was foolish to believe I could elude him forever, but *ugh*.

It was hard to believe we'd gotten to the point where we hadn't had a substantive conversation in nearly ten years. His dad's death was a seismic shift in our lives: Zeke lost his family's protector and provider, and I lost my best friend to grief. I did everything in my power to maintain our friendship during his first year of college. When my last texts went unanswered I gave up.

I felt hurt and resentful. His actions felt like a rejection—of our friendship, of our budding romance, of me. Grief drove his actions in those early years and he put up a wall around himself. The only way forward was to move on with my life. Without him.

I'd dreamed of giving Zeke a piece of my mind. Maybe this was my chance to find closure at last.

I see the sharp curve in the creek, the halfway mark in my route. My stress levels feel untouched, so I continue around the wooded corner.

Wham!

I hit what feels like a semi-truck and collapse like a ton of bricks. I'm falling backwards before I have a chance to react, and I brace for impact on the hard ground.

Something breaks my fall before my head hits. My vision swims, but I can see a pair of dark brown eyes looking into mine.

"I'm so sorry. Are you OK?" a deep, masculine voice asks with concern.

I think I've had the wind knocked out of me, because I can't form words to respond. Warm, strong hands support my back and head, likely preventing me from being knocked out.

"You're hurt. Hold still, OK?" The voice smells of soap and cedar, and is attached to a pair of muscular arms that easily scoop me up. I may be small in stature, but I'm athletic and strong. I'm not used to being dead lifted off the ground.

He sets me carefully on a tree stump, kneeling in front of me with both hands on my shoulders, and I look up. *Shit.*

"Hey," he says quietly. "Can you see me, Gen?"

I can mother-flipping see that the brick wall I ran into was Zeke Jacobs. And he's somehow five hundred times hotter than the last time I saw him up close.

"I'm all right," I wheeze, breath coming back into my lungs. I try to stand up and instantly get light-headed.

"Whoa, whoa," he grabs me around the waist and firmly sits me back down.

I huff in exasperation. "I'm just a little woozy." I lean around him. "I lost my phone and my headphones."

"I'll get them. You stay here." He looks into my eyes and I scowl. "Stay," he repeats with a smile.

He jogs off towards the trail and I exhale. What are the chances of literally running into Zeke? I'm annoyed at how attractive I still find him, which is a most unwelcome development in my plan to pretend he doesn't exist. He's gotten broader in recent years, seemingly putting on another 20 lbs of muscle. That explains why an unintentional body check sent me flying.

I'm standing up carefully when he gets back with my missing items. "I told you to stay put," he chastises, handing them to me.

"Thank you. I've got to get going," I state, brushing off the dirt and wood shavings from my lower half.

He runs a hand roughly through his hair. It's longer than it used to be. His natural waves fall around his forehead. "You can't keep running."

I pop my headphones back onto my head. "I can. I'll be fine."

He folds his arms across his expansive chest. "Don't be stubborn. What if you hit your head on the ground?"

"I'm fine," I repeat shortly and take two steps away from him.

Zeke cups my elbow, and I turn towards him in annoyance. My skin sparks where his palm lingers.

"Let me drive you home. I'm parked close by."

"Thanks, but I'm good."

He steps closer, bending his head down to mine. His clean and woodsy scent causes my insides to melt. I nearly drop my phone again in surprise.

"Would you rather I carry you?" His eyebrow arches in a challenge.

I scowl at him.

He smiles back, eyes sparkling.

I glare harder. *Dammit.* He's not bluffing.

I briefly consider the thought of getting thrown over his shoulder and carried home. He's already picked me up like I weighed nothing today. My cheeks warm and I notice him glance at them before coming back to my eyes.

Is he...flirting with me?

My brain fights to decide whether I'm angry or turned on. I embrace the safer bet.

"Fine," I respond with venom, ripping off my headphones. "You can drive me home."

Chapter 5

Zeke

I'm really racking up the wins this afternoon. So far I've managed to:

- Unearth repressed memories of Genny

- Go for a run

- Plow into Genny like a rampaging bear and nearly give her a concussion

- Flirt like an unsocialized teenager

- Piss Genny off

We walk to my car in silence, my mind racing to find something to talk about. She was clearly furious with me and I couldn't put my finger on why. Her sharp tone and flashing eyes were at odds with our accidental collision. I've only ever known her to be happy to see me. This Genny couldn't wait to get away from me.

She was still so damn gorgeous. The past ten years have barely touched her, as though I'd conjured her from the pages of my yearbook. The feel of her in my arms awakened senses I had long retired. I want to hold her in place and discover what's different since the last time I held her close. I want to trace every new crinkle around her mouth, and every curve of her hips. I wonder if she's still ticklish at her waist, and if she still listens to the Black Keys and Fall Out Boy. I wonder if I could ever make her smile again. My heart lurches painfully with the realization that I'd missed her.

I jog ahead of Genny and open the passenger door for her. She grumbles her thanks under her breath and gets in.

"Where do you live?" I ask, buckling my seatbelt and putting the car in gear.

"I'm out by the Community Center," she replies, looking out the window. "I'll let you know once we're close."

I inhale deeply for strength and catch the scent of her. She smells like vanilla, tangerines, and fall air. My stomach flips and I exhale shakily, keenly aware of how close we are in my old pickup truck.

She looks over and now it's my turn to ignore her, fighting a flash of desire and keeping my eyes trained on the road. She turns back towards the window and her long ponytail shimmers in the sunlight. I bite my lip and suppress the image of wrapping that hair around my hand and pulling her to me for a kiss.

Dammit. I really need a personal life. And probably a therapist.

I pull into Genny's driveway a few minutes later. If she could've tucked and rolled out of the car before it stopped moving, I think she would've.

"Thanks for the ride," she calls, the passenger door already halfway shut behind her.

"I–"

I sigh, running a hand through my hair in frustration as I watch her walk up her front steps. I feel a pang at the sudden loss of her. I'm reaching for the gearshift when I hear a knock on my window. I look up in surprise and come face-to-face with Genny. She makes a winding motion with her index finger, and I roll down the window..

"Hey," she smiles sheepishly and leans on my door. "I'm – Thank you for helping me today. And for the drive home."

My gaze gets caught up in hers and I can't look away. How is she even more stunning than when I last saw her?

Her eyes change and I realize she's waiting for me to reply. I clear my throat and look away. "No problem. I'm sorry I ran you over."

A tiny smirk plays at the corner of her mouth. "Yeah, well, maybe wear a flashing sign or something. *Linebacker Incoming.*"

I chuckle and let my head fall back against the headrest. "I'm really, really sorry."

"I know."

We look at each other for a few long seconds. She smiles tightly and raps on the door. "Well, see you around."

I watch her until she's inside her house, wondering, for the first time in years, what could've been.

Chapter 6

Genny

Avoiding Zeke is a full-time job.

Ever since our literal run-in I've been too spooked to run along the creek. I've visited the gym at odd hours (6am lifting session, anyone?) or worked out at home. Every time I leave the house, I worry that I'm going to see him somewhere along the way. My brain feels frazzled, unable to process life in its usual way, and I'm grumpy about it.

My thoughts keep returning to the memory of Zeke coming to my rescue. He'd been so gentle for such a giant of a man. He recognized me right away and still took great pains to make sure I was safe. I would have expected him not to care much based on our most recent interactions.

Much to my chagrin, I found it really freaking hot to be taken care of by him. I'm usually the one fussing over everyone else in my life. Getting literally lifted off the ground and made to take a break felt really, really good. It was easy to fall down the rabbit hole of imagining all the other ways he could take care of me.

"You're acting like you're in the Witness Protection Program," Mackenzie scoffs at me after school one night. "Let's get out of the house tonight."

"Don't feel like it," I mutter, roughly scrubbing the kitchen sink.

"Genesee," she cautions with annoyance.

"Mackenzie."

She disappears into her room for a few minutes, returning clad in athleisure. "Come on. Let's go to Pow Wow Fitness at the Community Center."

"I–"

"Men aren't allowed there," she reminds me pointedly, "so you don't have to worry about seeing Zeke."

I drop the sponge and huff. She's right, and moving my body would feel great right now. I'm tense and irritable, signs that I'm not getting enough movement in my days.

"You and Zeke should just hook up and get it over with," Mackenzie suggests as we walk into class, offloading our belongings into the provided cubicles.

"*Kenz,*" I hiss under my breath, shooting her a murderous look.

She shrugs and takes a swig from her water bottle. "That's what this is. You two never got a chance to be together all those years ago, and now you're both pretending you don't want to smash."

"Mackenzie Skye!"

"What? Zeke's hot, and you haven't gotten laid in *for.ev.er.*"

My face flushes and I pointedly turn away from my sister to stretch out my quads. She's not wrong on either count.

"Are you talking about Zeke Jacobs?" a voice cuts in behind us and I whip my head around.

Mackenzie, to her credit, looks sheepish as a group of younger women lean in. I recognize them from last month's Harvest Ceremony.

"Uh–"

"Oh my gosh, I heard he's moved back home now that he's playing for the Outlaws," a second woman gushes. "I've been going to the gym just hoping I'll run into him."

That makes one of us.

"He's so good-looking, isn't he?" the original woman sighs.

I smother a giggle behind my hand and catch my sister's eye. Zeke certainly has aged well. His six-foot-two frame has been filled out with delicious muscle and tattoos. He kept his hair buzzed short as a teen, but his current dark waves made me long to tangle my hands in them.

Traditional smoke dance music pumps out of the speakers as our instructor sets up. We file into the dancing space while chatting animatedly and bouncing lightly on the balls of our feet.

"You better snag him before some young hussy does," Mackenzie waggles her eyebrows at me and I laugh.

I didn't want to admit how good it felt to be around Zeke again last week. I had been crawling out of my skin to get away from him, of course, but he was warm and teasing. For a moment I could pretend we were 16 again.

Almost. Not quite. I suppose my life would be infinitely easier if Zeke and I could be friendly to each other again. Was friendship still on the table for us? It felt impossible after everything we'd been through, but I'm unwilling to write it off just yet. I was clearly still attracted to him, which was unfortunate. Maybe that would fade with exposure to him? I was on edge about seeing him after years of avoiding him, but surely that would fade with time.

I hop from foot to foot, spinning with the flow of the music as class begins. Mackenzie was right, much as I was loath to admit it. It was good for me to get out of the house.

"Could we stop by the fabric store on the way home?" Mackenzie asks as we're leaving class. "I wanted to sew new covers for the couch pillows over Thanksgiving break."

"Sure. I'll come wander around with you," I agree, and we set off.

My sister heads for the bolts of fabric while I roam the nearby aisles. There are always great craft supplies here that I can use with my students in future projects. I pick up some small acrylic paints and start walking in Mackenzie's direction.

I stop when I see a familiar linebacker browsing the rows of textiles. I back away quietly and zip down an aisle, hiding behind some garish Christmas decor.

What the heck is Zeke doing here?! My pulse races and I take a few breaths, trying to send word to my body that I've seen my ex-friend and not a saber-tooth tiger. I smother a cough as the cloying aroma of evergreen-scented candles invades my lungs.

I hear Mackenzie exclaim in surprise and assume she's just seen him. I inch as close as I can while still maintaining my defensive position next to the snowman wreaths. A bough of fake greenery pokes me and I swear. I'm shamelessly eavesdropping and don't care who sees it, as long as it's not Zeke.

"I wouldn't have expected to see you here," my sister teases. "Making your own lacrosse pinnies?"

Zeke chuckles. "My mom needed a few things for a sewing project, so I said I'd pick them up for her."

He's so damn considerate.

"Is Genny with you?" he asks, and I hear the hesitation in his voice.

I bite my cheek, praying Mackenzie has the good sense to lie through her teeth.

"She's not."

I owe her dinner tonight.

"Ah, OK," Zeke says. "How's her head? I ran into her last week, not sure if she mentioned it."

I press my lips together to keep from laughing. My sister has heard nothing *but* rehashings of our collision.

"She's good. No long-term effects." She pauses. "Do you need help with fabric? You look lost."

"I have no idea what I'm doing," he admits sheepishly.

Damn. He's cute when he's clueless.

I chuckle and tip toe away in search of a better hiding spot.

Mackenzie finds me in the far corner of the store a few minutes later. "Tell me you did not just run and hide from a man in a craft store."

"I absolutely did."

She groans. "The two of you are exhausting. Do we need to wait for him to leave so we can sneak out of here?"

I nod vigorously.

She huffs and leans against the wall. "He asked about you."

"I know."

"Of course you eavesdropped."

"Naturally."

She creeps away and peeks towards the front of the store. "He's checking out."

"Good." We stand in silence and boredom, looking around at the random clearance items in this part of the store.

"You can't keep avoiding him, you know," Mackenzie says quietly.

I sigh. "I know. But for now, I think I need to." I shuffle my feet. "It's too dangerous to be near him."

"You still love him." She pronounces it as a statement, not a question.

"I can't think that," I shake my head with a whisper.

She squeezes my hand. "Even if it's true?"

I wince. "Don't joke."

"I'm dead serious, little sis."

I rub my forehead, feeling a headache brewing from all of the scents assaulting my senses.

Mackenzie peers at the checkout lanes again. "All right, Pink Panther, the coast is clear. Let's get out of here."

Chapter 7

Zeke

The Outlaws' season is rapidly approaching, and preparations are intensifying.

We're entering our last weekend of training camp. Workouts are a top priority as players fight for final roster spots. Wes wanted to hit the gym tonight, so I dragged myself out past my bedtime.

My mind wanders as I load a barbell with plates. I think back to the months after my dad's unexpected death from cancer. In my shock and devastation I nearly backed out of my scholarship to Johns Hopkins University. The thought of leaving my grieving family to play lacrosse felt impossible and irresponsible. My brothers were young, and my mom was reeling.

My memories from that time are hazy. I had a clear recollection, however, of sitting on a park bench in late July. I stared at tree branches rustling in the breeze until the sun was low on the horizon. I didn't hear Genny approaching until she sat down next to me. My heart jumped at her presence, but emotionally I felt numb. I'd lost the ability to feel anything other than grief and anxiety over my impending departure for Baltimore.

She laid her head on my shoulder, threading her arm around mine so she could rest her hand on mine. She didn't speak for a while, and my shoulders slowly relaxed for the first time in six weeks. I hadn't seen her much since the funeral. I'd been doing my best to avoid everyone except my family. I couldn't summon the energy to answer any more questions about how my mom was doing or when I was leaving for college. How could I explain that I couldn't look forward in a world without my family's rock? The unknown was suffocating. How could I describe the weight of responsibility I now felt on my shoulders, as the eldest son, to be the protector and provider for those left behind?

"It's OK to not be OK," Genny whispered, her fingers interlacing with my own.

"But it's not," I snapped, shaking my head. "My family needs me right now, and I'm supposed to walk away from them and go off to play lacrosse two states away?" I bit my lip to suppress the rage and fear boiling up inside me.

"Live the life the Creator intended for you. That's the best thing you can do for your family," she insisted. "That's the life your dad wanted for you."

I closed my eyes, breathing erratically from rising emotions. I'd never felt this out of control and it was terrifying.

"Have you thought about talking to someone? I think a therapist could really–"

"No," I cut her off. "I don't need anything like that."

She wrapped both hands around mine, squeezing so hard it should have hurt. Instead, it felt soothing to my frayed nerves.

"We'll care for your family. The community will keep them protected for you." She firmly kissed my upper arm and my heart skipped a beat. "I promise."

The song on my playlist changes to loud rock, jolting me back into the present. I shake my head to clear it. The dream of Genny had died along with our canceled prom date. *Then why couldn't I stop thinking about her?*

"Good workout?" Wes asks, wiping his face with a towel as we're packing up our things.

"Yeah," I respond, gulping down water. "But I'm too old to be out this late," I tease.

We're making plans to carpool for a preseason game when we pass a group of young women.

"Hi, Zeke," one of them purrs, looking up at me.

I smile uncomfortably. I have no idea who she is. "Hey, how's it going?"

"Are you on your way out?" She pouts and her friends giggle behind her.

"Yeah, we're just leaving now." I clear my throat awkwardly. "Well, have a nice workout."

"What the hell was that?" Wes asks with a laugh once we reach our vehicles. "Did you know those girls?"

"I'm pretty sure I don't," I admit, reaching into my front seat for two post-workout shakes I brought for us to share.

"Thanks, man." Wes clinks his bottle against mine before taking a swig. "Well, *I'm* pretty sure they were hitting on you."

I blink in confusion. "What? No."

"Dude, how long has it been since you've tried to snag a woman?" He chuckles, shaking his head. "They were absolutely hitting on you."

I take a drink of my shake. My lack of flirting prowess had been on display with Genny earlier this month.

"A long time," I confess. "I've had a couple of girlfriends, but to be honest, my heart wasn't in those relationships. I shouldn't have gotten involved when my mind was elsewhere."

Wes takes another long sip. "Your mind was elsewhere, or your heart was?"

Damn, man. That was an unexpected shot across the brow.

I exhale. "Probably a bit of both."

He raises an eyebrow at me as he finishes his shake. "Maybe it's time for you to try again."

I chuckle. "You come to the rez and start acting like an uncle already?"

Wes throws his head back and laughs. "The sacred wisdom just starts flowing. What can I say?"

I toss my empty shake into my truck, along with my bag. "All right, Medicine Man, I'll pick you up around five on Friday, OK?"

"Sounds good, Z. See you then."

I reflect on Wes' question as I drive home. Was my heart elsewhere in my prior relationships? The chemistry always felt incomplete. I never felt what I felt for Genny with anyone else. That was a painful realization, considering it had been ten years since we'd last spent meaningful time together. I continued to be largely uninterested in dating. My capacity to love felt like a switch in the 'off' position, and no one else knew how to turn it back on.

Did I still love Genny? My memories of the first year after my dad's death weren't the clearest, but I knew I hadn't been a good friend to her. I would guess that contributed to her recent coldness towards me.

I sigh, my heart heavy as I arrive home.

Chapter 8

Genny

"Chels!" I exclaim with delight, standing in the doorway and holding open my arms for my longtime friend.

Chelsea runs into them and squeezes me tightly. "I'm so happy to see you! I'm seriously in need of girl time."

Chelsea had bounced around between her dad's house in Cattaraugus and her mom's near Utica, NY. We'd spent our high school years thick as thieves playing lacrosse and getting up to no good together. Chelsea, Mackenzie, and I loved spending time together when our schedules aligned.

I welcome her inside my house as Mackenzie comes around the corner.

"Kenzie!" Chelsea pulls her into a hug. "Look at you with the deadly auntie earrings. I love them." She cups her hand and traces the ridges of my sister's beaded hoop earrings.

"I know. Aren't they great?" Mackenzie strikes a pose.

"Do you want drinks while I start dinner?" I ask, grabbing her duffel bag and bringing it into the living room.

"Hell yes!" Chelsea and Mackenzie reply in unison.

I grab wine glasses from a cabinet while my sister procures a chilled bottle of white wine.

Chelsea slides a chair up to the counter and plops down, gratefully accepting a beverage. "I needed this," she sighs.

"What's up?" I ask, laying out a baking mat and rolling pin. I made pizza dough yesterday in anticipation of Chelsea's visit.

She gulps her wine. "I called things off for good with Brock."

Mackenzie and I both murmur various combinations of "oh, no," and "I'm sorry."

Chelsea chuckles. "You don't need to pretend. I know you both hated him."

"Brock? That angel?" Mackenzie bats her eyelashes innocently.

Brock is a lacrosse player from Toronto who plays for the team in Albany. He's handsome, talented, and an absolute waste of space. He treated Chelsea badly behind closed doors. She is a force to be reckoned with, and her light has dimmed since he's been in the picture.

"I know I shouldn't have stayed as long as I did." Chelsea looks into her glass. "He's an asshole. But I thought it was my fault that he was that way."

Mackenzie and I spring into action, piling onto our friend and enveloping her in a hug.

"Don't you dare let that dipshit make you insecure," I insist.

"He's not worth the price of your beadwork, girl." Mackenzie squeezes her tightly.

Chelsea smiles weakly. "Thanks, friends. I know you're right. I just need a break from men." We slowly release her and grab our own glasses to clink against hers in agreement. "Especially lacrosse players."

"For real." I take a sip in solidarity.

"Speaking of lacrosse players to avoid," Mackenzie elbows me, "are we watching the Outlaws preseason game tonight, or boycotting the season?"

I sigh heavily and Chelsea tilts her head in confusion.

"What's this?" she asks.

"Zeke is on the Outlaws now," Mackenzie answers, "and he nearly knocked Genny unconscious last week."

Chelsea spins to look at me, her eyes wide. "Zeke Jacobs?"

I nod, biting my lip.

"He's back living on the rez, then?" she surmises, and I nod again. "I think we're going to need more wine for this."

Chelsea had been there with me through the Zeke drama. She understands what a blow it is for me to be living in the same spaces as him again.

"How are you feeling about this?" she asks, moving her glass out of the way as I roll out the dough.

I sigh, leaning into each roll. "Not great, honestly. I've already run into him—literally run into him, by the creek."

"And he looks *good*," Mackenzie adds.

Chelsea raises an eyebrow at me.

I twist the lid off a jar of pizza sauce and start spooning it onto the dough. "It's true. Unfortunately."

"Let me see. Where's your remote?" Chelsea wanders into the living room.

"Next to the couch," Mackenzie calls.

"Got it!"

I hear the TV switch onto the game. I'm sprinkling mozzarella cheese onto the pizza when Chelsea loudly exclaims.

"Holy shit."

I start to laugh. "What?"

"He's huge!"

We walk over to where Chelsea is gaping at the TV. Players are standing helmetless for the national anthems, including Zeke.

Seeing him in an Outlaws uniform leaves me breathless. We grew up watching games with our families, and the sight of him in the familiar orange, white, and black makes my heart race. His jet black waves fall into his eyes as he glances at the floor. He's absolutely gorgeous.

"Hot damn," Chelsea observes, still staring at the TV. "And you ran into him? How did you not die?"

I tear my eyes away from Zeke and walk back towards the kitchen. "I'm pretty sure he nearly gave me a concussion."

"And then he flirted with her," Mackenzie points out. I glare at her from across the room.

"I'm going to need all these details, please," Chelsea insists, following me back to her earlier position at the counter.

"You want pepperoni?" I ask, back to work on the pizza.

"Yes, please. Now what did Zeke do?" Chelsea presses.

"He, uh–"

"He told her he was going to forcibly carry her back if she didn't agree to a ride home," Mackenzie butts in, stealing a pepperoni off the top before I can stop her.

"Hey!" I swat her hand away.

Chelsea whistles quietly. "You should've let him."

"That's what I said!" Mackenzie agrees.

I finish sliding the pizza into the oven and around with a point in their direction. "Stop it, you two."

"I mean, if he needs a volunteer to pick up and throw around…" Chelsea trails off, waggling her eyebrows.

"Oh my God," I lean against the counter, my shoulders shaking from laughing so hard.

"In all seriousness, have you considered trying with Zeke again?" Chelsea asks gently a few minutes later while we watch the game and wait for the pizza to finish.

I shake my head, my eyes following Zeke as he maneuvers on the floor during a power play. "I don't think I can. I don't trust him anymore."

He catches a pass and out-muscles a defender, backing him up and spinning towards the goal. He shoots low and beats the goaltender. The crowd goes nuts, cheering for the goal as his teammates swarm him to celebrate. I smile sadly. It's the first goal I've seen him score since college.

The oven timer dings, and I hop up to retrieve the pizza. "Come on, let's eat!" I announce. "Chels, we're going to need the extra fuel if you want to go shoot around tomorrow morning."

"Heck yes," Chelsea responds. "Let the carb loading begin!"

Chapter 9

Zeke

I'm sore from last night's game, but ready to shake out my muscles. Wes and I are shooting around this morning, both of us eager to keep putting in work before the start of the season.

"How're you feeling today?" I ask him as we pull into the parking lot closest to the lacrosse fields.

He nods. "Good. Sore, but good."

I park my truck and look over at him. "I hope you're not feeling too discouraged after being assigned to the practice roster. It's a long season, and you're the best young defender I've seen in years. I know you'll be a starter soon."

Wes smiles warmly. "Thanks, Z. I'm not discouraged. I know I'll get there."

I clap him on the shoulder and grin. "You've got the right mindset and resilience to do it."

"This place looks great," he enthuses, looking around at the Cattaraugus Community Center.

"I spent a lot of time here as a kid," I explain. "The fields were an outlet for me when I needed a break from the chaos. I lived with three younger brothers." I grin.

He chuckles and grabs an equipment bag. "Thanks for inviting me out. I've been missing my Oneida community."

"Yeah, man. Come on out anytime. You're welcome here with your people."

We come around the corner of the building and the athletic field comes into view. A couple of women are shooting around and I frown.

"Should we go somewhere else?" Wes asks.

"Nah," I reassure him. "They might be finishing up, or willing to scrimmage with us." I smile and scan the field. My stomach drops when I realize that one of the women is Genny.

Shit. I haven't seen her since I ran her over two weeks ago, and I can't imagine she's going to be any happier to see me this time.

"Zeke Jacobs. Long time no see," Chelsea says with a smile when she notices me approaching.

Chelsea's mom is Oneida, so she mostly grew up in her maternal nation. She spent a few years living on Cattaraugus with her Seneca dad in high school. The three of us played a lot of lacrosse together during that time. She and Genny helped lead the girls' team to a state championship game our senior year.

Genny turns around to look in my direction. I observe the panic flash across her face when she sees me. *Dammit.*

"Hey, Chels." I take a few steps forward to pull her into a quick and friendly hug. "Nice to see you around here again."

"You, too. Genny told me you were back living on the rez." She looks over at a clearly uncomfortable Genny and flashes her an encouraging expression.

"Yeah, I've been back for a few weeks now. We're getting ready to start our season soon." I nod towards Wes. "This is my teammate, Wes. He's Oneida."

Wes smiles warmly at Chelsea, extending his hand. "Nice to meet you."

Chelsea raises her eyebrows and returns his handshake. "Chelsea John. I'm Oneida, too. Who's your family?"

"My mom's Kay Patterson, but she moved out to Wisconsin in the 90s. I'm not sure who's left in New York from our family." Wes shifts from foot to foot, his gaze downward. "We've never visited."

Chelsea lights up. "Of course I know who Kay is! Your grandmother is a Bear clan mother. Your cousin Jessica is one of my friends. I'll have to tell her I met you."

I glance over at Genny and catch her looking at me. She smiles nervously and looks away. I take the opportunity to check out her long, athletic legs in black running shorts. I recall how they looked draped over my forearm as I carried her away from the trail two weeks ago. *Damn.*

I glance back at Wes, who is beaming at Chelsea.

"I've got a cousin my age?" he asks with a grin.

"Dude, you have so many cousins," Chelsea emphasizes. "You should come visit!"

"Maybe I will."

"Would you ladies be opposed to playing pickup ball with us?" I ask, hesitant to interrupt. I'm thrilled that Wes is already making connections.

"Not as long as you don't mind getting your asses handed to you," Chelsea teases. She elbows Genny, who still hasn't said a word.

Wes gives her a lopsided smile. "Bring it on."

"I'll set up the goal," Genny offers, spinning to head towards the net.

I open my mouth to speak but she's gone. I watch her walk away, feeling the weight of her continued absence.

"Give her time," Chelsea says quietly, scooping up a loose ball.

I look at her in surprise.

"She's still hurt, dumbass," she raises an eyebrow. "You were really shitty to her."

I forcefully exhale. "I know."

She taps my stick with hers. "*Do* you?"

Wes covers a laugh with a heavy cough, reaching around me to grab the equipment bag. I narrow my eyes at him and he mouths "I'm sorry" before heading towards the field.

She watches him walk away before turning back to me. "Let's go, dummy. I think we've all got some aggression to work out."

Wes is helping Genny rig a sheet of plywood down the center of the net, simulating a goalie since we don't have one. I notice her smile as he talks to her, and her laughter floats over as Chelsea and I approach.

Am I going to have to kill him? I couldn't remember the last time I made Genny laugh.

"Do you want to play with pads?" I ask.

"Don't have any," Chelsea responds. "Why, are you afraid we'll hurt you?"

Wes chuckles under his breath.

"If you want us to go easy on you, just say so," I reply with a teasing grin, dumping lacrosse balls out of my duffel bag.

"Simmer down, hotshot," Chelsea grabs a ball and places it in the middle of the field. "Let's do this."

"You cover Chelsea," I tell Wes. "You're our best defender, and she's squirrelly."

"I can imagine." He looks over at where she and Genny are strategizing.

"I've got Genny. I know how she plays."

"I don't know that this approach is going to help your case with her, man. I've seen you with women."

I fix him with a pointed look, and he grins.

"Just promise me you won't be a shitass." He winks.

"I'll do my best."

Genny and I park ourselves behind Wes and Chelsea as they set up for a faceoff. She still hasn't said more than five words in my vicinity.

"Gen," I whisper loudly while we wait, and her eyes dart over in surprise, "you OK?"

She blinks at me and then nods her head. "Yeah. I'm OK."

I smile hesitantly. "I promise I won't bulldoze you again."

Her eyes lighten. "You better hope I don't try to get even."

"I hope you do."

Dammit, Jacobs. Stop. Flirting.

"Down. Set. Go!" Genny calls towards the faceoff circle.

"Z!" Wes' voice rings out and I look up to see he's flung the ball in my direction.

I take a couple of steps back, stick at the ready. Suddenly Genny flies in front of me and snatches the ball away before it can land in my mesh.

"Goddammit," I mutter, stopping my backward momentum so I can chase her.

Chelsea calls for a pass, but Wes has her well covered. Genny looks over, then turns back to the net. I slash my stick across hers to try dislodging the ball, to no avail. I gain the last step I need to catch up to her and block her forward progress. She huffs in frustration before throwing her body sideways into mine.

"I'm not as easy to push around as I used to be," I quip, barely moving.

"Neither am I." She looks me directly in the eyes and my heart skips a beat. She flicks her stick in the opposite direction, sending a perfect behind-the-back shot sailing into the net.

Chelsea yells in jubilation and runs over to celebrate.

Wes walks over, and we watch the girls hugging and giving each other high fives.

"When I said don't be a shitass, I didn't mean let her run all over you," he deadpans.

"Yeah, yeah," I grumble, heading back towards the middle of the field.

It was my turn to face off next. I can hear Genny breathing heavily as we lean closely together over the ball, waiting for the call from Chelsea. She smells like oranges and fresh grass, which distracts me from my focus. *Some things never change.*

"Go!"

Genny reacts a split second faster than I do, the head of her stick falling on top of the ball. We wrestle for control, my stick covering hers and our knees bumping against each other.

"Fuck. Off," she grits out, trying to wrench her stick out from underneath mine.

"Not a chance," I breathe near her ear, leaning in harder.

"Hey! Hurry it up, you two!" Wes calls out.

Genny swears and throws her body towards my shins. She tilts my balance enough that her stick head pops free.

"Dammit," I growl, my torso crashing onto hers as she swings her stick and pushes the ball out to a waiting Chelsea.

She rolls away from me, attempting to get to her feet. My hand juts out, grabs her right foot, and pulls. She falls again, swearing profusely.

"That's a fucking penalty," she kicks at me and I dodge, laughing.

"And who's going to call it?" I grin.

She opens her mouth to spit back a response when we both hear a skirmish erupting nearby.

Chelsea, with no one to pass to, is playing keep-away with Wes, dodging and bobbing in her attempts to get to the net. Wes stick-checks her and otherwise blocks her with her body, grinning as she heckles him.

"What's wrong, rookie? Don't want to play rough with a girl?"

He grins. "You want to play rough?"

"With you? Hell yeah." She winks and shuffles to her right.

I scramble to my feet, narrowly avoiding a heel to the chest from Genny. "Don't let her get in your he–"

Wes falls for it, over-committing to Chelsea's dodge and unable to recover when she spins out in the opposite direction. He falls on his ass as she runs around him, scoring easily.

Genny whoops from the ground, arms raised in victory as Chelsea jogs over to high five her.

Wes sits on the grass, laughing to himself as I make my way over to him.

"She's a master trash talker, man." I shake my head.

"I see that," he chuckles, watching Chelsea help Genny up from the ground.

The four of us play together for over an hour, with a lot of sweating, laughing, and grass stains mixed in. It feels so good to laugh with Genny again. I'd forgotten how mesmerizing she is when she laughs with her entire chest, her eyes crinkling with unrestrained joy.

Once we're exhausted, she helps me retrieve balls from the field and deposit them into my equipment bag. We chat easily for the first time in years. My heart aches in an old and familiar way that is deeply uncomfortable.

"I guess you got even," I smile, zipping up my bag.

She fans her flushed face with her hands, her sweatshirt long abandoned and her shoulders glistening with sweat. I clench my fists to cut off an image of pulling her back against my chest and running my lips down the column of her neck.

I snap out of the fantasy and realize she's looking at me expectantly. "I'm sorry. What'd you say?"

"I said, your teammate is nice," she repeats, squirting water into her mouth from her nearby bottle.

"Yeah, Wes is great. I'm trying to get him to come out to events here. I think he feels out of his element, growing up removed from his mom's family." I squint at where he's talking to Chelsea.

"Well, he fits right in," Genny smiles. "If he can put up with Chelsea, then he's one of us."

I gesture to our friends with my chin. "We might need to worry about those two."

She chuckles. "I don't think so. Chels is pretty solidly in her Single Girl Era."

Wes and I load up my car a few minutes later, and he looks happier and more relaxed than I've seen him.

"You seem happy," I smile, getting into the driver's seat.

He leans his head against the back of the passenger's seat. "I am. That was fun."

"It really was."

"So what's with you and Genny?" he asks.

My hand stills on the gearshift. "Nothing. We're friends. I think."

"You think? What kind of answer is that?"

I look over, and Wes is staring at me pointedly.

"You're up to your fucking uncle shit again, man. You're so damn nosey."

He lets out a hearty laugh, and we hit the road.

Chapter 10

Genny

Gakwi:yo:h Farms is bustling with activity.

Our annual husking bee is one of my favorite events. My people come together to prepare Haudenosaunee white corn to be dried and processed for our ancestral foods. We nearly lost this important food due to European colonization. The Senecas led the way in protecting heirloom seeds and educating communities on how to grow, pick, and process them. Each year's husking bee is a celebration of our people's resilience. I love using my hands to shuck and braid the corn. It connects me to the earth and our traditional ways.

Groupings of hay bales are arranged in the barn so families can sit together and work. My dad and Mackenzie head over to the mound of corn in the back, while my mom and I set up an assortment of baskets.

"*Nya:wëh sgë:nö*', Faith and Genny."

I look up to see Zeke's mom, Elaine, smiling widely in greeting. Her mother-in-law, Delores, is with her.

"*Hae'*, Elaine and Delores." My mom embraces her longtime friends. "*Sadögweta'*?" she asks with a squeeze.

"I'm feeling good." Elaine replies with a grin. "Especially since the full wolf pack is home again." She gestures behind her to the gaggle of tall, dark, and handsome Jacobs boys trickling into the building. Zeke has brought Wes along as well, and they're working together with his brother Jordan to load up baskets of corn.

"Come join us," my mom encourages, gesturing to our circle of hay bales.

I smile in agreement while groaning internally. I had a great time playing lacrosse with Zeke the other day. Too good of a time. I let down my guard and found myself enjoying his company. The banter between us had been easy and familiar. Being in his presence made my body come alive. His smiles made my stomach flip and my breath catch. Wrestling with him for the ball had left me warm and wanting more.

I absolutely, positively, could not afford to fall back in love with Zeke. I wouldn't survive him breaking my heart again.

The sound of heavy baskets hitting the ground pulls me from my reverie as everyone returns laden with corn.

Wes plops down between me and my mom, and I breathe a sigh of relief that Zeke will sit on the opposite side of the circle. We exchange friendly smiles and greetings as he introduces Wes to my family.

"So, Wesley," Elaine grabs an ear of corn, "we grew this corn using heirloom seeds that are at least 1,400 years old. Each time we remove the dried kernels, we save some for future plantings."

Wes whistles in appreciation, and I hand him and Mackenzie some corn to get started. I have to smack my sister's arm with it to get her attention as she's exchanging flirty glances with Jordan. Those two have hooked up over the years, and it seems like we're entering another cycle of it.

Elaine, Delores, and my mom show Wes how to prepare the corn, pulling the husks and silks down. The excess husks are ripped off and tossed into a basket for use later in the braiding process. The silks are placed in a separate basket.

"You can make tea from these," my mom says, shaking some sticky silks off her hand and into the container. "They're nature's way to balance blood sugars and stay healthy."

I use a handheld tool to cut the hard ends off the corn. They fall to the ground with a satisfying *thunk*. Ezra, Zeke's youngest brother, is chatting with him and my dad about his classes, and I raise my eyes to tune into the conversation. Ezra is in his final year of college, and I know how hard he's worked at his academics to get here. He's always looked up to Zeke, and his brother's experience as the first person in their family to get a college degree was an inspiration for him.

Zeke pushes up the sleeves of his gray knit sweater as he husks, and I exhale a shaky breath. His forearm tattoos peek out as his strong hands deftly pull down husks and silks. The man has no right to be as gorgeous as he is.

He glances over at me and our eyes catch. I was blatantly ogling him, and I freeze in surprise.

Shit.

He smiles slowly and warmly, his eyes drinking me in.

My stomach flips in response, and I drag my gaze away. I notice Wes silently focused on husking and turn my attention to him.

"It seemed like you and Chelsea got along well the other day," I say to him with a smile as I continue snipping off hard ends and tossing them into a basket.

He smothers a grin and clears his throat, jiggling a handful of corn silk off his hand. "Yeah, I think so." His cheeks flush the barest shade of pink and I hold back a delighted giggle.

Chelsea insisted she's not interested in dating any more lacrosse players, but I could tell she liked him.

"Chelsea John?" my mom asks, and I nod affirmatively.

"Did you get her number?" I ask, grabbing another ear of corn. I glance up and catch Zeke still looking at me. I quickly look away.

Wes smiles wider. "She wouldn't give it to me."

I laugh, because of course she wouldn't. "Do you want me to give it to you?"

He shakes his head, eyes sparkling. "I'll get it, eventually."

I guffaw. "I like your confidence."

I notice Zeke still looking my way, and I'm annoyed. "What?" I mouth at him silently.

He shakes his head quickly and looks back down at the half-shucked corn in his hands.

It's so strange to see Zeke looking at me again with life behind his eyes. For years he'd look straight through me, barely acknowledging my presence. His current friendly overtures felt hollow. Where was this during the past ten years? What was different now? Didn't he realize how empty his friendliness was? My decade-long anger simmered at the surface, close to overflowing.

"Gen, could you pass me some more corn?" he asks, interrupting my emotional spiral.

I use my foot to wordlessly shove over the basket closest to me.

"Thanks," he murmurs, and I feel a sting of regret at my rudeness.

Chapter 11

Zeke

"We're almost done," Miles observes, looking behind the hay bales for additional corn.

"There are a few baskets in the drying room that got left behind," Genny's mom, Faith, says, snipping off a hard stem.

"Zeke, could you help Genny grab the rest?" my mom asks, gesturing with her chin towards the opposite side of the barn.

I groan internally. Genny has been short with me all afternoon, any progress we made playing together this weekend seemingly gone.

"Wes, would you mind coming to help?" I ask him, eager to have someone around to cut the tension.

He nods, but my mom stops him from getting to his feet.

"I'm going to teach Wesley how to braid the husks together." She looks up at me pointedly and I catch her intent. Genny and I need to work this out together.

Wes mouths "sorry" at me and turns towards my mom for his lesson.

I stand and hold my hand out to Genny to help her up. She ignores it and breezes past me..

"You were really shitty to her," Chelsea had said to me over the weekend. I know I'd let our friendship falter, but did I really comprehend just how badly I'd treated Genny?

My mind cycles back to the night my dad died. My mom and I were getting ready for prom: finding a suit without wrinkles, buying flowers for Genny, and taking out cash from the ATM. It was a hard time for our family, but we were making the best of it. My dad had been diagnosed with advanced cancer two weeks prior. His prognosis was poor, but he had a chance. While we were gone, he collapsed at home, and a panicked 15-year-old Jordan had to call an ambulance.

He was gone just a few hours later.

I remember my mom's anguished wail as he slipped away. My youngest brother was only 11, and she was left to raise four boys on her own. Despair fell over my grandparents, especially my grandmother, at losing their son before he turned forty.

Genny's family was waiting for us when we got home late that night.

"Your mom called," Genny whispered, wrapping herself around me. "I'm so sorry, Zeke."

The atmosphere was funereal as relatives swirled around us. Some aunties and uncles took the younger boys for the night, while Faith and Jerome comforted my mother and grandparents.

"I don't want to leave my mom," I insisted. "I don't want her to be alone."

"She won't be," Genny reassured me. "And you won't be, either. We'll stay as long as you need us."

Family and friends filled the house until well past midnight to offer condolences and support. I became increasingly more overwhelmed by the number of people stopping by and talking to me. Genny tugged me outside into the muggy June air, and I gratefully followed her onto the back deck.

"Let's take a break," she said, sitting on the porch swing and pulling me to her. "There's a lot going on inside."

She opened her arms and I fell into them, the pent up anguish of the day spilling out.

"What am I going to do without him, Gen?" I sobbed. "We need him."

She held me tightly, her fingers gripping my back. "I don't know," she admitted, "but we'll figure it out together."

I clung to her like a life raft. She was my port in this storm of unfathomable intensity.

"I'm so angry." I shuddered against her. "Why did this happen? Why would the Creator take him away from us?"

She ran her fingers through my short hair as I buried my face in her shoulder. "I wish I understood it," she said. "I wish I could take this pain from you."

"He's supposed to watch me play at Hopkins," I cry. "He was so proud of me."

"He still is," she said. "He always will be."

I alternated between crying, yelling, and throwing things off the deck. Genny welcomed me back to her arms in between outbursts, never afraid of the strength of my vacillating emotions. She stayed by my side for hours until I could no longer fight sleep.

That was the last time I cried. The dawn brought with it a new feeling—numbness. I had a laser focus on what needed to happen each day: help my mom, comfort my brothers, thank the hundreds of people who came by to mourn and fill our fridge and freezer with food. This one-foot-in-front-of-the-other survival strategy lasted well past my college years. Sometimes I think I really only came out of it within the past year. I had put the family on my back for so long that I hadn't realized they could now stand on their own. It was time to put them down and work on my own healing.

Perhaps part of that was repairing the ruins of my relationship with Genny.

The animated hum of the barn brings me back to reality. Genny and I silently walk together towards the storage room where we will later hang the braided corn to dry for several months. It's a long process from first planting to enjoying a steaming bowl of corn soup.

In front of the drying racks, there's a small trough of fresh ears still waiting to be sorted and shucked. Genny grabs a basket and starts roughly tossing corn inside like it owes her money.

Now's your chance.

I take a deep breath and crouch near her with a second basket, slowly placing individual ears inside. "Gen, I'm–" My mouth feels like cotton.

She slowly turns to look at me curiously. "Are you all right?"

I nod, wetting my lips. It's now or never, and I may as well just jump straight into the fire.

"I don't know where to start," I admit, looking down at the basket, "but I know the end point is telling you how very, very sorry I am for…" I look up and gesture back and forth between us. "…this."

She freezes, her eyes fixed on me. "For what?" Her voice is barely above a whisper. I think she may have stopped breathing, based on how still she is.

"For walking away from my best friend ten years ago," I respond. "I don't–I can't explain why I pushed away everyone in my life, especially you, after my dad died. I know it was the grief, but that's not an excuse for how I treated you."

She's still staring at me, motionless.

"You've always been there for me," I rush forward, feeling spooked by her silence. "I didn't appreciate you. I ghosted so many of your calls and messages." I hang my head in shame. All of this feels far too little, too late.

"You broke my heart."

Her words slice through me, spoken plainly but firmly. She stands and I look up at her. Her eyes shine with unshed tears.

"I loved you. I would've done anything for you," her voice wavers slightly. "I kept all my promises to you, and you just…forgot about me."

She loved me. My world tilts at the revelation. I'd been in love with Genny my entire life, and still was if I was being honest with myself. Never once had I considered that she might feel the same way about me. She'd loved me and I'd screwed it all the way up.

"I deserve that." I swallow painfully. "But I want you to know I never forgot you. Never. I often wished I could have forgotten you."

She growls with frustration and begins to walk away.

I close my eyes and take a deep breath to steady myself.

"Ow!" Something hits me hard in the shoulder. "What the–" I look and see Genny glaring at me, her eyes furious. At my feet is an ear of corn that wasn't there before.

"Did you just...throw corn at me?" I ask in shock.

She has the good sense to look embarrassed, but it's clearly a secondary emotion after rage. "I did."

"Ancestral corn? Food of our people?" My lips quiver upwards.

"The ancestors are mad at you, too," she spits. "I'm sorry you couldn't forget about leaving our friendship for dead."

"Do you want to take this outside, tough guy?" I smile weakly, my heart in tatters at the magnitude of my sins.

Genny walks away again before spinning on her heel and stomping back. "Why now, Zeke? You haven't given me the time of day in ten years. Why? Now?" She chucks another ear of corn at my feet, her face full of anguish.

She doesn't deserve this. I should've left her alone instead of hoping she would give me a chance after what I did. It's impossible to stitch a fatal wound closed.

I shake my head sadly, knowing that any words I could share wouldn't be enough.

She blinks away tears. She silently turns back towards the trough of corn.

"I loved you, too," I breathe, the words out of my mouth before I can stop them.

She stills. "I know."

I bark out a surprised laugh. "Was it that obvious?"

"Yes."

We get back to work filling our containers, an uneasy quiet between us.

Genny stands, hoisting her basket up into her arms. She's about to leave and take my heart with her.

"Do you think you could ever love me again?"

She pauses at my question, her chest rising and falling with slow breaths. "I don't know," she eventually admits.

I nod slowly, the dimmest sparks of hope stirring in my heart. "That's generous."

She closes her eyes and inhales before heading back to our families.

Chapter 12

Joto:h

When it's cold

Genny

I peel rambunctious students off of each other - again - and direct them back to their desks. I hear a crash and a wail behind me as I pull up our daily math lesson.

It's every teacher's worst nightmare: the dreaded wait between Thanksgiving and winter break. My students are bouncing off the walls, because today is a school assembly and Winter Field Day. They'll try different sports and hopefully burn off some of their excess energy.

It also means, unfortunately, that I have to see Zeke.

The school is surprising students with an Outlaws clinic given by Wes and Zeke. It's an opportunity to encourage kids to try lacrosse and move their bodies.

I am dreading seeing him again after our conversation at the husking bee. Argument? I wasn't sure what to call it. Since I threw something at him, it felt like more of an altercation than a cordial chat.

Chucking corn at him wasn't my finest moment, but damn, it was satisfying. I had been so frustrated with him for so long. Hearing him attempt an apology had brought out a level of rage I didn't realize I still had. What the heck was I supposed to do with his empty words after all this time? He couldn't saunter back into my life and expect to be friends again like nothing happened.

It's time for the assembly. I line my students up outside our classroom, and we process to the packed gymnasium. Everyone is buzzing with excitement, as they've heard we have some surprise guests. I smile at my students' vivacity and joy, reminded again of how grateful I am to do what I do.

"And now," our principal says with a grin, "I am excited to introduce you to our special guests. We have two players from the Buffalo Outlaws here to talk to us about the game of lacrosse and the benefits of team sports."

The students whisper animatedly to each other.

"Let's give a warm welcome to East Lake Elementary's very own Zeke Jacobs, from the Seneca Nation, and his teammate Wes Harrison, from the Oneida Nation."

The gymnasium erupts with applause. Outlaws players are local celebrities around here. They're heroes, most especially, to the large contingent of Indigenous students who attend our school.

Zeke and Wes enter, wearing orange Outlaws practice shirts and black shorts. Feelings of pain and confusion lodge themselves uncomfortably in my chest.

They share what lacrosse means to them, especially how physical fitness has positively impacted their lives. Wes talks about the importance of taking care of our bodies so we can be our best for others. I notice Zeke's gaze drifting around the large room while he speaks.

I keep my eyes fixed on Wes, smiling at his words and occasionally glancing over to shoot some whispering students a withering stare. I glance back and catch sight of Zeke looking right at me. I blink in surprise, and he gives me a hesitant smile. I slide my eyes immediately over to Wes.

This is going to be a long day.

Following the assembly, we break up into grade levels and start moving through the Field Day circuit. Fifth grade goes outside to play basketball for twenty minutes. We then relocate to the cafeteria for some karate instruction from a local teacher. I break up multiple sets of students karate chopping each other.

We rotate again, this time back to the gym for lacrosse. I take a deep breath before entering.

The gym is divided in half, with mini orange cones arranged in patterns on each side. Large plastic bins are filled with black lacrosse sticks.

"Hey Genny!" Wes smiles and fist bumps me as I walk by with my class.

"That's Miss Skye to you," I tease him, my eyes sparkling.

"Of course." He laughs and steps aside. "Are you kids ready to play some lacrosse?" he asks the room with a smile.

Zeke stands next to him, shifting back and forth on his feet. He looks over at me.

"Hey," he says quietly.

"Hey," I respond.

Wes blows his whistle. "Let's get you into two large groups. Students over here with me will be practicing ground ball pickups and defensive maneuvers." He gestures to the area closest to him with his stick. "The rest of you will be learning how to pass and catch with Zeke."

The whistle sounds again and we split up our classes. Much to my chagrin, Wes' side fills up quickly, so I bring my students over to Zeke for our first session.

"Hi, everyone. We're going to have a lot of fun today," he grins. "Who has played lacrosse before?"

Approximately half of the students' hands go up.

"That's great! You'll be able to help your classmates who have never played." He rolls over the nearby bin. "Come grab a stick, and then stand next to one of the orange cones. I'll show you what to do next."

The kids eagerly rush forward to grab sticks, spinning them in their hands as they find an available spot to stand.

"Just remember, sticks are *not weapons!*" I call out over the din, anticipating the inevitable chaos.

The students arrange themselves in two parallel lines along the cones. They each have a partner across from them, and a healthy distance in between.

"Place your right hand at the top of the stick, and your left hand at the bottom." Zeke demonstrates. "If you're left-handed it's the opposite. Bend your arms and hold them away from your body."

I walk down the lines while he's talking, helping reposition small hands to the correct places.

"Now *push* the stick with your top hand, and *pull* with your bottom hand. See how that feels?" He shows them the motion and watches as they mimic him. "Good! Try to smooth it out into one motion. That's how you pass the ball."

He scoops one up with his stick and turns to face the padded gymnasium wall. He throws the ball and it hits with a *thunk*. It bounces back and he catches it. "Catching it is just the reverse. *Pull* with the top hand, and *push* with the bottom hand. Let your stick come back towards your shoulder as the ball lands."

The kids move their sticks forward and back, practicing the mechanics.

"Gen—Miss Skye," Zeke's voice startles me, and I look over. "Would you mind passing with me so we can show them what it looks like?"

His face is hopeful, and I resign myself to the task. "Sure."

He hands me a stick and our fingers brush when I take it. A zap of electricity flows between us. I keep my eyes down, afraid to catch his glance for fear he felt it, too.

I back away, putting distance between us so we can safely throw. I wing up a prayer to Creator that my moccasins don't slip on the shiny gymnasium floor. It was a Casual Friday, so I wore jeans and a soft black turtleneck. Should've worn sneakers...oops.

We pass back and forth as Zeke talks the kids through how hand position makes the movement more accurate and strong.

"Remember that lacrosse is good medicine," he teaches, catching the ball and switching to his backhand to send it back to me. "It's hard to feel angry or sad when you play. The game helps you heal yourself and your relationships with those you play against. We play to honor the Creator and those who came before us."

"Miss Skye, I didn't know you could play lacrosse!" one of my students says.

I chuckle and catch the pass. Zeke is making me look good because he's so accurate.

"She's really talented, too," Zeke chimes in with a smile. "Did you know she went to the State Championship with East Lake High School?"

"Whoa!" The fifth graders are suitably impressed, and my cheeks flush from the attention.

"You've got a superstar teaching you," he says. "She should be the one leading these drills."

There goes my heart again, cracking open and spilling onto my moccasins. *Why does he have to be so damn* nice?

Zeke comes over while I'm monitoring the kids passing and catching. Missed balls are rolling across the floor while students dodge passes to retrieve them.

"Maybe we should have started with wall ball." Zeke frowns.

"I could've told you that."

He chuckles and rests the end of his stick on the floor.

"You still keep me on my toes. You're a hell of a player." He glances at me. "I really enjoyed playing with you again."

I avoid looking at him, keeping my eyes on my gleeful students. "You may be bigger, but I'm craftier."

He laughs. "That's true. I might need you to teach me a few new tricks this season."

I smile but keep my head turned away from him.

An uneasy silence falls between us as he shouts out words of encouragement to the various groups.

"You seem happy," Zeke says quietly to me. "Your life is full and meaningful."

I nod. "It is."

It's silent again, and I look over to find him watching me.

"I'm really happy for you, Gen," he says, his voice low.

"Thanks," I smile thinly, feeling like an imposter. My life is full and meaningful, but true happiness is still something that I'm chasing. Something is missing, and right now it feels like *him*.

His eyes are sad as they look into mine. I find myself holding my breath, uncertain of what happens now. I don't know how to feel around him anymore. Are we friends? Are we enemies? Are we acquaintances who don't really care much? None of those options sound appealing to me.

He gives me one final half-smile and blows his whistle, gesturing to Wes to collect the kids and switch groups.

"Thanks for your help today, Miss Skye," he says.

I watch him walk away and my heart aches.

Chapter 13

Zeke

"**Z**eke!"

I scoop up a ground ball and turn toward my mother's voice. "Yeah?"

She's leaning out of her back door, calling across the yard to where I'm practicing wall ball against the side of the garage. "Your grandmother just called. She's running low on firewood and there's a cold snap coming this weekend. Could you get her set up before you leave town?"

"No problem. I'll do that now." I climb the exterior stairs to my apartment, leaving my stick propped against the inside door frame. We have our first home game tomorrow against Albany, and I'm heading to our team practice in a few hours. I gather some supplies and head out.

My grandmother's house is only a few minutes' drive from mine. I've been meaning to go over there and finish stocking her firewood supply for the winter. Training and the team have been keeping me busy. Still, that's no excuse, and I feel a pit of guilt in my stomach as I pull into her driveway.

She steps out of the house as I'm unloading my truck. "*Nya:wëh*, Ezekiel. Thank you so much. I know you're leaving soon for Buffalo, and I hate to inconvenience you."

"You're never a bother, Grandma," I reassure her, giving her a one-armed squeeze. I take care to keep my axe angled away from her slight frame. "You can call me anytime, and I'll be here." My grandfather passed away a few years ago, and my family pitches in to make sure she has everything she needs in his absence.

Her chestnut eyes twinkle as she looks up at me. "You're always there for everyone. I hope you're taking time for yourself, too." Her warm hand rests against my cheek before patting it lightly. "Come inside for some corn soup before you start."

It's a request that is not up for discussion. I stifle a sigh as I follow her inside. I'm happy to be there, but I'm eager to get started. I know it'll take several hours to bring in the wood she'll need and chop a bit more to dry.

"Sit," she commands kindly, gesturing towards her kitchen table with her chin. "It's getting cold out there, and you need something warm in your stomach before you work."

Her house is chilly, and the guilt flares back up in my chest. What if she's been conserving wood because it was running low? I should've been here weeks ago. Heck, I should've spent longer when I first started stacking and chopping logs for her winter supply. *I can't believe I didn't–*

"Here you go." My grandmother looks at me warmly but firmly, jolting me from my spiraling thoughts. She sets a steaming bowl of corn soup in front of me. I smell the delicious aroma throughout the house from where the pot sits simmering on her wood stove. I smile gratefully and thank her, breathing in deeply as I stir the bowl to release some heat.

"I may have called you over here on false pretenses."

A heaping spoonful of soup is halfway to my mouth and I stop at her words. I look up and smile. "What do you mean?" My frown returns in the next instant. "I'm sorry. I know I should've been back a while ago to finish bringing in the rest of the wood. I'll make sure you're taken care of to–"

"Zeke." The firm tone of her voice gives me pause once more. "I have plenty of wood to get me through the weekend. Or I could've asked one of your brothers to stop by."

I take a bite of soup and hum appreciatively as the delicious warmth floods my insides. My mom's corn soup is amazing, but my grandmother's is next level. I shake my head and swallow. "It's my responsibility, and I didn't do a good enough job the first time. The boys are busy, and I can split wood twice as fast as they can."

She places her hand over mine before I can take another spoonful. I let go of the spoon and nudge the bowl to the side.

"I'm sorry. I'm not being a very good listener, am I?"

A smile edges along the corner of her mouth. "Your father wasn't either."

A sad smile passes across my face at the mention of him. "No, I suppose he wasn't."

"I invited you here because I wanted to talk to you," her voice drops lower and my heart sinks. "This has been going on for a long time now, and I'm worried." The bottom falls out of my stomach as I anticipate her next words.

"About you."

Huh?

I blink at her in confusion.

"I'm worried about you," she repeats, squeezing the hand she's holding. "I've tried to guide you over the years and give you time to feel the grief of losing your dad. But Zekey, I'm afraid if you keep going down this path, you'll get stuck there forever."

My head swims. "I'm not sure what you mean, Grandma. Everything is great with me."

"Is it?" Her eyes meet mine and I feel deeply uncomfortable. My family typically avoids addressing the elephant in the room—my mental health. "I saw how you and Genny were at the husking bee last month."

I feel my heart beating slowly, so loudly that it rushes in my ears. I don't know what to say in response. I pride myself on staying so consistently busy that I never have time to sit and think about my life besides doing more - more workouts, more volunteering, more errands, more everything.

But that's what I have to do. That's what's expected of me. I have a responsibility to my family, to my team, to the kids on Cattaraugus.

My grandmother squeezes my hand again, sensing my mental spiral happening. This time, her grip is less firm and more comforting. "I see you, Ezekiel. I see the storm behind your eyes. You're a good man who puts family and community before all else. You're an inspiration to all the *Onödowá'ga'* kids here who see what you've accomplished as a Seneca."

"But underneath all this tough stuff," she raps against my chest, "I know you're still a scared and devastated boy who's just lost his father."

My eyes flutter shut, unexpected tears pricking at the corners. I'd shoved my emotions to the side since that tragedy, but I was starting to crack. I've spent ten years chasing greatness in order to provide for my family, and it never felt like enough. *I* never felt like enough.

My grandmother cups my cheek and brushes a tear away with her thumb. "You've been taking care of us for a long time now, Zeke. And I want you to know how much we appreciate you and love you. And that it's OK to turn that back over to us and find some of your own happiness." She smiles, full of love and encouragement. "We're safe. You're safe. That little boy is safe here."

"Grandma, I can't..." my voice chokes, and the emotion I'm holding back bursts through unabated.

She holds me until the storm passes. Her grip is tight around my back, and I gradually soften in her arms. My thoughts are cloudy, but I'm surprised to feel physically lighter, as though I've just shed a 90lb weighted vest.

"Finish your soup and get some wood chopped," my grandmother insists, pushing the bowl back towards me. "You'll sleep well tonight."

Chapter 14

Genny

I'm exhausted after a long week. There's one more day until the weekend, and I need to rally.

Every Thursday, I go shopping for myself and Zeke's grandmother. She calls me the night before to tell me what she needs, and I pick up her items while I'm at the store. It's an easy way to make sure she's taken care of and save the Jacobs family some time.

I'm anxious to get Delores' groceries inside so I can head home. A cozy night in with a book and an early bedtime is just what I need.

I swear when I see Zeke's car parked in my usual spot. *Of all the times for him to be visiting his grandmother!* I'll need to make this a quicker trip than usual.

"*Hae'* Dee Dee!" I call while backing into her front door. My arms are laden with grocery bags.

"*Nya:wëh sgë:nö*', Genny," she smiles at me from her perch next to the wood stove. She's stirring a huge pot of what smells like corn soup.

I turn my head slightly so I can scan for signs of Zeke in the small house. *Nothing.*

I exhale and head straight for the kitchen. I dump the bags on the vinyl floor and get right to work unloading the perishable items.

"Have some corn soup once you're done," Delores insists, gesturing with her wooden ladle towards the table.

"I'd love to, but I can't stay long today," I admit ruefully. Delores' corn soup is the best in Cattaraugus, and everyone knows it.

She nods understandingly. "I'll pack some up for you to take home, then." She meanders over to the cupboards in search of a container.

I close the fridge door once I finish. Next up is sorting through everything else. I glance out the window above the sink and nearly drop a can of kidney beans.

Zeke is out back, tossing cut pieces of wood into a pile. He's rolled up the sleeves of his flannel shirt to his elbows, and I can see flashes of his tattoos peeking out from underneath. He wipes his forehead and surveys the remaining logs to be split.

I hear Delores' voice behind me and struggle to pull my eyes away. "...isn't that right?"

I turn my head towards her guiltily. She'd filled a glass container with heaping spoonfuls of soup. "You have a half day tomorrow, right?" She snaps the lid in place and slides to me.

"I do," I answer with a smile. I'm grateful for a simple response after being caught gawking at her grandson. "Parent-teacher conferences are in the afternoon." I bring my attention back to gathering the canned goods and organizing them into her cupboards.

I fold up the brown paper grocery bags. "I'll throw these into the recycling bin and then I've got to head out. I'm sorry I can't stay longer." I sneak another glance out the window and swear quietly under my breath. Zeke has unbuttoned his maroon flannel to reveal a white shirt underneath. He sizes up a log before raising his axe and swinging it down with a tremendous *whoosh*. I gulp. *Hot damn.*

"No problem, dear. *Nya:wëh* for the groceries this week."

I spin back around to find Delores with mirth sparkling in her hazel eyes. I smile and give her a hug goodbye, hoping to hide the blush that I feel flaming across my cheeks. I'm heading to the recycling bin when she stops me.

"Oh, one last thing."

A sense of impending doom rumbles past me. "Sure, what's up?"

"Since you're heading towards the backyard, could you bring this cup of tea out to Zeke? He's chopping wood, and it's gotten so cold in the last hour. He could use a warm up."

Delores hands me a mug of tea. I look at it like it's an undetonated bomb. My eyes lift back up to hers, and that absolute hellcat of a woman is grinning at me. She knows exactly what she's doing.

"I, uh..."

"I would do it myself, but my knee is bothering me." She hobbles forward a step, and I reach out to grab the mug from her and steady her. "Must be this cold weather moving in."

"Mmm hmm," I see that the sparkle has not left her eyes. "Come sit down and I'll run this out to Zeke." I help her over to the table, knowing full well that she has the both of us wrapped around her finger.

Once she's settled, I take a deep breath, roll my shoulders back, and open the back door.

Chapter 15

Zeke

I've refilled the wood rack and I'm splitting a half dozen logs to dry for later. My head is clearer. I've worked out some anger and frustration with the axe, although I can feel the need for rest creeping in. I don't want to overdo it this close to a game.

For the first few logs, I thought about my family. About how much everyone has grown, and how strong my brothers have become. I haven't wanted to admit it, and I've continued to push back against relinquishing any leadership opportunities to them. The reality is they've been helping my mom steer the ship for years, especially Jordan as the second-oldest. He has a good head on his shoulders. He's calm, intelligent, and has an eye for the emotional needs of others. Miles is a balanced partner for him, although he's still rash on account of his youth. Ezra has been working his tail off in college, and I am so dang proud of him. The four of us have grown up a lot together in the past ten years.

My thoughts eventually turn to Genny, and with my defenses lowered she quickly consumes me. Watching her with her students tugged at my heartstrings. She'd always wanted to be a teacher, and she achieved her goal. I hadn't been there to witness her accomplishment. I feel a pang in my chest as it dawns on me just how much I've missed since I left home as a teen. She's lived a life without me, and she's moved on.

If I could release the unshakeable need to be everything for everyone, what would my life look like? Could I allow myself to hope that something remained of what Genny and I once shared? Could she ever trust me again?

Thwack! I swing at a log again, feeling entirely too warm from the past hour of work and the uncomfortable sensation of my emotions running amuck. I peel off my outer shirt and toss it aside, enjoying the coolness of the air on my bare arms.

I follow through on my last swing and hear an almost imperceptible intake of breath. I look up and there she is, her eyes traveling down the length of me before crawling back up to meet mine. My own breath catches, and the mask I've clutched in place for so long falls.

Chapter 16

Genny

I just need to say hello, leave the tea nearby, and hightail it out of there. I can handle that.

I take slow and careful steps towards the spot where Zeke is splitting wood. I'm trying not to alert him to my presence until the last moment and hopefully avoid unnecessary small talk. I have to keep pausing every few steps, however, because he is being *so damn hot.*

He takes off his flannel shirt and I nearly trip over a tree root. His biceps ripple as he raises the axe and swings it down forcefully. I close my eyes for a second and try to gain control over my heart rate. I'm stuck inside a TikTok thirst trap and it is exquisite agony.

He's put on at least 30 lbs of muscle in the past few years, and his cotton tank shows every one of them. God bless America.

Zeke has always been a good-looking guy, but adulthood and a professional training regimen have chiseled his features.

He's still the boy I loved, but his confidence and experience have matured him. He's gorgeous, funny, and kind, a lethal combination for me at this stage of my life.

With a deep and silent breath I continue forward. I desperately wish I could teleport home immediately or invent an invisibility cloak so I could watch him. He must be deep in thought, because he hasn't noticed me yet. After another hard swing, he grabs the bottom of his shirt and pulls it up to wipe his forehead. The brief flash of his abs short circuits my body.

I breathe in sharply, my brain scrambling and my hormones spiraling. It proves to be my undoing, as my eyes lock with his on their languid trip back up the contours of his torso. It's the last breath I take for several seconds as we stare at each other, and I know my desire for him is plain as day on my face.

"Gen," he breathes, a wide grin breaking across his face. "You're here."

I stand there like a doofus, holding a steaming mug of tea and possessing zero coherent thoughts. He hasn't looked at me like that since we were seventeen. I don't know how to respond, too afraid to believe this is real. He's gorgeous, breathing heavily, and smiling at *me*.

Chapter 17

Zeke

Seeing Genny is like waking up on Christmas morning. And unless my radar's broken from ignoring it for so long, she's unabashedly checking me out.

My insides warm as my smile spreads. I'm not sure how long we stare at each other before I notice the goosebumps on her forearms, and my brows furrow in concern.

"You're cold." I step forward and instinctively grasp both of her arms with my hands. She shudders at my touch, and my eyes drag across her towards the sloshing cup of liquid in her right hand.

"I'm not. I was just–"

I hardly ever see Genny flustered. She's always calm and confident, the way I've tried to be in my adulthood. She could have been such an incredible support in my life if I would have let her.

I release her and go in search of the flannel shirt I'd chucked to the side earlier. I shake it out and turn back towards her. "Here. You're shivering."

"No, no, I–"

I drape the deep red fabric over her shoulders, fighting the urge to pull her close. Her long chestnut hair hangs loose underneath.

"Zeke, please, I'm just trying to–"

"Let me take this from you." I wrap my hand around the mug she's holding.

"Yes, thank you! That's what I've been trying to give you." She pulls my shirt off as I set the cup down on the ground.

"You haven't been trying very hard." My eyes twinkle as I take the shirt from her and wrap it back around her shoulders. She glares up at me as I gently push her down onto a nearby tree stump. "Sit and warm up."

She huffs as I retrieve the mug of tea and place it back into her hands, crouching down to wrap my own around hers. "You are your grandmother's grandson."

I smile as we both look at our hands folded together. My emotional dam is breaching and I think I don't give a shit.

"What are you doing here?" I ask, my thumb rubbing across the back of her hand. "Besides delivering tea, of course."

She shivers again, and I resist the urge to bring her hands to my lips for warmth.

"I was bringing your grandmother her groceries."

I raise my eyebrows. "That's really nice of you. I'm sure she appreciates that."

"I do it every week, dumbass."

I burst out laughing at her insult. "You do?"

"Yes. I've done it for years."

"Seriously?" I sit back, letting go of her hands. "How did I not know this?"

Genny looks down at the mug. "I think you've missed a lot."

A few seconds pass between us in silence, my heart aching. The scales have fallen from my eyes, and I'm ready to take a chance.

I scoot forward on the ground in front of her and wrap my hands back around hers. "Would you consider coming to my game tomorrow?"

Her eyes look over to mine in surprise.

"I know we haven't—Gen, I've fucked this up so much," I stumble over my words. "I know I don't deserve any more of your time, but I would be honored if you'd come see me play. It's a home game, and you could hitch a ride with my family."

She searches my eyes and I'm afraid to look away.

"It's been a long time since I've gone to one of your games," she says quietly.

"It has," I reply tentatively. "That's my fault, and I want to make it right."

She looks down at my hands for a long while.

"I'll think about it," she finally responds.

I exhale the breath I've been holding. "Thank you."

She stands and hands the tea to me. "I need to get going. Thanks for letting me borrow this." She shrugs off my flannel and I realize just how much I enjoy seeing her in my shirt.

She finishes gathering herself and heads back towards my grandmother's house, my eyes following her every step of the way.

Chapter 18

Genny

My hands shake as I drop bags of groceries onto the kitchen table.

Mackenzie emerges from her room when she hears me. "There you are! Let me grab the rest from the–" She sees my face and stops. "What happened?"

I pull out a chair and plop down. My head falls into my hands.

My sister sits next to me, her face etched with concern. I give her an overview of my experience with Zeke at Delores' house. I'm too close to the edge of letting my feelings for him out in the open, and I don't know how to proceed.

"Go to the game," Mackenzie urges.

I groan. "If I go, then it gives him a signal that I want more with him."

"Well," she says, opening a package of grapes from the groceries and popping one in her mouth, "don't you?"

I run my hands through my hair in frustration. "It doesn't really matter what I want. It's a bad idea."

"Why?"

I comb my hair over my shoulder so I can braid it and have something to fidget with. "You know why!"

Mackenzie chews another grape. "Do *you* know why?"

"Why are you talking in riddles?!"

She chuckles. "You may think you know why you shouldn't get close with Zeke, but I think you're just afraid to get hurt again."

I stare at her like she has two heads. "Of course I'm afraid to get hurt again. I don't trust him not to drop me at the first sign of hardship in our lives."

"There!" Mackenzie points. "That's it! That's what you need to tell him."

I tilt my head in confusion.

"I love you, Genny. You're the most forgiving person I know." She squeezes my hand with a smile. "I know you'll eventually forgive Zeke, because that's who you are. But being able to trust him is something only he can show you. And he needs to know that."

I nod, my fingers reaching the end of my braid.

"I think he deserves a chance to prove himself to you," she says quietly. "He's a grown man now, and he seems to realize how his grief poisoned your friendship. It's clear as day that he still loves you and wants to make it right."

"You really think so?" I ask, an edge of hope sneaking into my voice.

"The whole damn rez sees it, girl," she replies pointedly. "Now, go call Elaine before it gets too late. Find out what time she's heading to Buffalo tomorrow."

Chapter 19

Zeke

The locker room is buzzing with activity. Teammates chatter animatedly, equipment is velcroed on, and helmets *thunk* against wooden stalls. It's the first home game of the season. Everyone is excited to welcome back the rabidly loyal fans, as well as play in front of family and friends.

I left five tickets for my family at Will Call. My mom loves coming to games and bringing along various combinations of people with her. I knew Jordan and Miles were planning to come with her tonight, and I was hoping Genny would join them.

I figure the chances of her coming are low, but I'm holding onto a shred of hope.

I pull on an orange Every Child Matters warmup shirt. Outlaws players wear them to raise awareness of U.S. and Canadian residential schools. These schools removed Indigenous children from their communities in order to separate them from their culture. Sales of the shirts are a fundraiser for a national healing initiative.

"First game in The Hideout, that's a big deal," Sawyer says, referencing our arena while tying his sneakers in the stall next to mine. "Well, first time playing for the good guys, that is." He winks.

I chuckle, tugging an elbow sleeve into place for shooting support. "The home locker room is pretty nice, I have to admit."

"Don't let it make you soft like Lanes," Jamie taps Sawyer on the head. "He's gotten too used to the finer things in life."

"Let's get warmed up, boys!" Coach Travis calls from the hallway. I quickly grab my helmet and stick.

We run onto the floor together as a team. It's early, but I can't help but glance at the section where my family sits. No one's there yet.

Players jog around in circles, taking turns shooting on the net to warm up our goalie. It's also a chance to try out a new move or trick shot.

I scan the stands and see my mom walking to her seat with Miles right behind her. I smile and wave at them, trying not to be too obvious about looking behind them for anyone else.

"Z, you're up!" Sawyer taps me with his stick and I jolt back to reality, scooping up a ball. I approach the goaltender slowly, faking like I'm shooting low between his pads. I quickly change course and shoot over his shoulder.

He makes the save and I mutter to myself. It wasn't my best effort, and I'm distracted.

Sawyer, Jamie, and I huddle together to try out some plays we worked on in practice last night. Sawyer is determined to make a hidden ball trick work one of these days. It's an attempt to confuse the other team so they lose track of the ball. It rarely works, but it's fun to try.

The warmup playlist switches over to a slower song. That's our cue to stretch. The lower bowl of the arena is filling up with excited fans taking pictures and video. Dusty, the Outlaws' opossum mascot, comes up to some of them for high fives.

Jamie and I peel off to work through our stretching routine. We know each other from years of Haudenosaunee National lacrosse teams and community events, so we chat easily.

"Is your family coming tonight?" I ask.

"Yeah. My parents are making the drive from Six Nations with the kid," he replies while stretching his arm across his body. "Hopefully they don't have any trouble." He grins. "My dad likes to rile up the Border Patrol agents by showing his Indian Status card instead of his passport."

I laugh. "There's never a bad time to remind them of their border crossing treaty obligations." Being a pain at the Canadian border is a national pastime for Haudenosaunee people.

"You're damn right."

We transition to the ground to stretch out our hip flexors. It's a bit of an awkward position to be caught locking eyes with a random fan, so I typically look at the ground in front of me during this portion. I'm anxious to check my family's section again, however, so I can't resist a quick peek up into the seats.

She's here.

Chapter 20

Genny

Well, I'm here.

Elaine was thrilled to hear Zeke had invited me to the game, and insisted that I bring Mackenzie along with us. Ezra was back at college, so she had two tickets available. I dusted off my old Randy Bissell jersey for the occasion. He was a Tuscarora Nation superstar for the Outlaws back in the 1990s. I paired it with a short, black corduroy skirt, fleece-lined black tights, and combat boots.

Butterflies riot in my stomach as we enter the arena. Jordan, bless him, offers to buy us drinks to take back to our seats. His easy smile and conversation helps take the edge off my nerves.

"Over here," he says, indicating with his head.

We follow him to the family's section, clutching beers in our hands. The teams are warming up, and I carefully descend the steps in front of me. Jordan slides in next to Miles, and I let Mackenzie go first so she can sit next to him. She hasn't said anything to me about it, but I had to squeeze next to those two in the back of Miles' car on the drive up. They flirted up a storm.

"Do you see Zeke?" Mackenzie asks me.

I take a sip of my beer and scan the floor. The players are stretching, so it's hard to tell who's who. I look over at the area directly in front of us and find myself staring straight at Zeke. He's leaning forward on his knees, dynamically stretching his hips and groin. I choke on my beer, coughing roughly.

"You OK?" My sister pounds on my back before following my eyes to the floor. "Oh, Jesus."

We watch the players stretch, sipping our drinks with interest as they change positions. Zeke sees us at one point and smiles broadly. Mackenzie waves on our behalf as I sit frozen by her side.

I loosen up a bit after my drink, which is a relief as it helps me enjoy the game. Zeke still plays the same. He's electric on the floor: easily dodging defenders, making buttery smooth passes, and burrowing himself into holes near the net. His shot is hard and deadly accurate. His increased size means he can knock down other players and bully his way around more than he used to. I have to admit, it's hot as hell watching him topple grown men with his body.

He scores two goals in the second half, one of them an impressive behind-the-back shot that fools the goaltender. It's a bittersweet joy to celebrate with his mom and brothers again, the five of us high-fiving and yelling his name.

The Outlaws win the game by five goals. The arena explodes with cheers as the team makes a loop around the floor, their sticks raised to the fans once the clock expires.

"Let's go find Zeke," Elaine calls down the row to us.

My easy-going attitude evaporates. I force a nervous smile and nod at her. In the haze of celebration and beer, I hadn't thought ahead to seeing Zeke after the game. Anxiety writhes in my gut as we gather our belongings and head out.

We slowly push our way through the throngs of fans spilling onto the concourse and towards the exits. I find myself separated from the rest of the group by surging crowds.

Elaine looks back and sees the distance growing between us as more people flood the space in front of me. She plants her feet and reaches back for me, eventually grasping my hand and holding tight until I'm able to pull closer.

"I don't want to lose you!" she smiles, draping her arm around me and squeezing. "We'll show you where the players meet up with their families and friends."

My own smile wavers. Another lifetime ago, I would wait for Zeke outside the high school locker room after his games. I'd had every expectation that the trend would have continued while he played at Hopkins. His invitations to games had dried up, however, after we graduated.

It wasn't for lack of effort from his family. Elaine encouraged me to travel with them to Baltimore every home weekend during lacrosse season, but I consistently begged off. The idea of seeing Zeke uninvited made me feel ill.

We approach a wood-paneled wall with the Outlaws' logo painted on it. The wall conceals a nondescript entrance. Players' loved ones crowd the inside of a simple room with names and photos of notable players in team history. We hang around the periphery, chatting and laughing while reliving memorable moments from tonight's game.

A second door opens and players trickle in. My heart thunders in my ears each time the door squeaks, a sickening sense of dread creeping over me. *What if Zeke isn't happy I'm here? What if his invitation was out of a sense of obligation after learning I brought Delores her groceries?* My throat tightens at the memory of the vacant stare he'd given me during his college years. I don't think I have the emotional fortitude to see that again.

I feel a squeeze on my hand. I glance over to find Mackenzie encouraging me with a soft smile.

"It's going to be OK," she leans over and whispers in my ear.

Tears prick my eyes as I nod in agreement, catching my lower lip beneath my teeth.

The door creaks open again and my head snaps in that direction. *Well, shit.*

Zeke strolls out dressed in a navy blue suit, his white shirt collar unbuttoned and his lacrosse stick in his hand. His tousled waves are damp from the shower. His eyes scan the room as a small group springs forward to request his autograph. Creator, help me. This man is *fine.*

Mackenzie nudges me and I realize I'm staring at him, frozen in place while Elaine, Jordan, and Miles move towards his position. My heart is now beating out of my chest, and each step feels like I'm wearing concrete shoes.

Zeke smiles warmly while he signs lacrosse balls and jerseys. He laughs easily as they congratulate him on a good game, and suddenly his eyes look up and latch onto mine.

"*Yo!*" Mackenzie hisses in surprise. She'd walked directly into my back when I stopped in my tracks. "What are you–"

Thump. Thump. My heart rate slows, pounding loudly in my ears as Zeke stares at me. Panic zips through my veins. *This isn't what he wanted.* I feel hot and dizzy, as though I may pass out.

I need to get out of here.

I'm about to flee when his face lights up with joy. His smile spreads to a grin, with his focus completely dialed into me.

"Oh, girl," Mackenzie chuckles and wraps her hand around my upper arm. "You are the only person in the room for that man right now."

My heart remembers what it's like to be caught in the sunshine of Zeke's gaze, even while my body trembles with fear. My pulse quickens as he glances back at the fans he was talking with. He wraps up the interaction while his eyes keep darting back to me.

"I'm so glad you came." Elaine smiles knowingly at me as Zeke approaches our group.

"Thank you for letting me tag along," I squeak out before this six-foot-two wall-of-man is standing in front of me.

Chapter 21

Zeke

Genny looks like a fucking dream, and I'm transfixed by the sight of her waiting for me.

I didn't think she'd actually come.

Her hair is loose, and it cascades over the shoulders of her vintage Outlaws jersey. Her black fringe earrings are tangled in her hair, and I desperately want to reach out and adjust the silky strands. I feel a primal urge to see her wearing *my* jersey.

"You came," I breathe, my eyes drinking her in.

She nods, her face drained of color.

I want to pull her to me for a hug and tell her how happy I am to see her. My brothers, however, come over to congratulate me.

"You looked great out there, Z." Jordan and Miles take turns clapping me on the back.

"I'm so proud of you, Zeke," my mom smiles and folds me into her arms next. "Welcome home."

I squeeze her tightly. "Thanks, Mom. I'm so thankful to be here."

"Not bad for a scrappy *Onödowá'ga:'* kid," Mackenzie teases, warmly embracing me once my mom has let go.

I chuckle. "Good to see you, too, Kenzie."

I look back at Genny, and she really looks unwell. I reach out and tuck her under my arm. "You OK?" I ask quietly, bending my head down to hers.

"I think I need some air," she whispers, looking nauseous.

"Let's get you out of here," I insist. "Do you want me to drive you home? You probably don't have room to breathe with five people squeezed into Miles' Civic."

She nods and sways on her feet. I tighten my grip on her shoulder to steady her.

We say goodbye to our families, with my mom handing Genny a bottle of water to drink. Mackenzie makes me promise to take good care of her sister. I lead Genny into the locker room, poking my head around the corner first to make sure everyone's mostly clothed.

Jamie is shrugging on his suit jacket and raises an eyebrow at me as I enter.

"Is Ted still around?" I ask, hoping the team trainer hasn't left yet.

"Yeah, he's in the back," he gestures with his head.

"Please, I don't want any fuss," Genny pleads weakly. For the second time in recent memory, I'm tempted to throw her over my shoulder and make her get medical attention.

We find Ted packing up the last of his equipment, but he immediately grabs his bag and comes over to evaluate Genny. I gently grip her waist and lift her onto the padded examination table. I crack open the bottled water and hand it to her.

Ted glances up at her in concern after taking her pulse, and I feel the blood drain from my face. *Please don't let this be serious.*

"Let's have you lie down with the fan on and see if that helps," he says kindly.

I grab the nearby box fan and prop it up on a counter. It blows directly on her while Ted tucks her coat and purse out of the way.

"Is that any better?" I ask her. I brush some damp tendrils away from her forehead. She feels clammy and I'm starting to feel sick with worry.

"It's still too warm." She's breathing heavily and her neck has gotten splotchy.

"Do you want to take this jersey off? I can make sure no one comes back here."

She nods and starts to slide her arms out from underneath the material. Her hands are weak and fumble with the fabric. "Can you help me?"

I take a deep breath and steel myself for the unexpected battle of helping Genny undress. She's trying to pull the jersey over her head, but she's sweaty and her hair is getting in the way. I gather her hair to one side and tuck it away beneath the jersey. I grab the bottom and gently peel it up and over her head. Much to my relief, she's wearing a black tank top underneath.

She lays down on her side and I bring the fan closer to the table.

I lean down and sweep some more hair from her face. "Do you want me to stay with you or give you space?"

"You can stay," she whispers.

I pull a folding chair over to the table. I sit and hold her hand, watching the rise and fall of her breathing gradually slow. Her eyes flutter shut and my breath catches.

She looks so peaceful as she rests, her hair waving in the breeze from the fan. *She's magnificent.*

It feels illicit to watch her uninterrupted, but I take the opportunity to re-learn every contour of her face. Her eyes eventually open and I notice some color has returned to her cheeks.

"Good morning," I murmur as she blinks at me.

She releases my hand and pushes herself up on the table.

"Whoa there, tiger." I stand and grab hold of her shoulders, which feel cool and dry.

"I'm OK," she assures me. She swings her legs over the edge of the table and sits up. I notice goosebumps on her upper arms and frown.

I immediately strip off my suit jacket and wrap it around her shoulders. "Is it too cold in here now?"

I lean to switch off the fan, and when I return she's breathing heavier again.

"What's wrong?" I ask in alarm, my hands on either side of her arms.

"Nothing's wrong." She inhales deeply. "Your jacket smells like you, and I'm finding it very overwhelming."

Her eyes lock onto mine and my breathing picks up. I unconsciously lick my lips and her eyes fall to them. My fingers grip her upper arms and I'm consumed with the desire to kiss her.

"How are we feeling, Miss Skye?"

I jump back from Genny at the sound of Ted's voice.

"Good. Better." She's blushing, and it goes straight to my ego.

He re-checks her pulse and looks her over. "You're looking and sounding a lot better. As long as you're feeling more stable, I'd say you're good to go."

I send Ted home with words of gratitude while I retrieve Genny's belongings.

"Do you want to wear my jacket home or change back into your jersey?" I ask. I allow myself a quick peek down at her all-black outfit with my navy blazer swallowing her frame. She looks fucking beautiful.

"I should probably give this back to you," she says quietly, looking up at me from where she still sits on the table in front of me.

I trace my index finger down the lapel, our heads close together. "You look good in my jacket," I murmur.

For a few seconds, all I hear is the sound of our breathing.

"Zeke." Her voice shakes.

"Yeah?" My fingers gently fist around the suit fabric. I won't kiss her unless I know for sure she wants me to, and right now it sure feels like she does.

"Z! You still here? I see your stuff in your locker."

I sigh heavily and pull back from Genny just before Sawyer comes around the corner. A blazing smile lights up his face.

I force a grin and raise my arm for a fist bump before a quick bro hug. "Hey, man. Great game. That was a nasty shot you scored on to put us ahead."

"Yeah it was," he laughs and claps me on the back. "I couldn't have done it without that perfect pass you sent me."

He looks over at Genny and the first beginnings of panic flutter through my abdomen. My eyes dart over to her as she smiles shyly in his direction. *Uh oh.*

Sawyer is one of the best goal scorers in the league, with an ego to match. He's flashy and brash, but deeply loyal and kind. The best kind of guy to have on your team, but the worst kind of guy to be grinning at the woman you're trying to win over.

I clear my throat and place my hand lightly on Genny's arm. "Sawyer, this is Genny. She's..." I pause awkwardly, suddenly uncertain of how to introduce her. *How do I describe who she is to me?*

"Genny." Sawyer smiles widely, reaching out to shake her hand and wrapping it up firmly. "Like the beer?"

She returns his smile, but I notice the slightest tightening of her mouth. She's heard that line about the local brewer, Genesee Beer, her whole life. He's flirting with her and she's...annoyed?

"Not really."

He hasn't let go of her hand yet and I'm two seconds away from stepping on his toes.

"So nice to meet you, Genny," he winks.

Genny pulls her hand away and reaches for her coat that I'm holding. "Oh sorry, I hear my phone. Let me see who's–It's my sister." She pulls her phone out and gestures into the locker room. "Do you mind if I take this?"

"Of course, go right ahead. I'll be right here," I let her know, smiling in relief as she tosses my blazer onto the table and begins walking away.

"Is that your girl?" Sawyer asks once she's a few paces away.

"No," I reply, trying to keep the hope and sadness out of my tone.

"Oh?" His expression perks up, eyes still glued to her in the next room on her more-than-likely fake phone call.

"Well–" I interject, panic fluttering in my midsection yet again.

He glances at me.

"She's, uh—"

His eyebrows creep upwards, the beginnings of a smirk playing at the corners of his mouth. "She's...?"

"It's complicated," I admit with a sigh.

Sawyer chuckles and elbows me in the ribs. "A pretty girl wearing your jacket usually isn't too complicated of a situation."

I grumble as we both watch Genny end her call and begin walking towards us.

"Well, she's gorgeous and unfortunately not interested in giving me the time of day, so I think you should *un*-complicate things with her," he joked.

Chapter 22

Genny

What. Am. I. Doing?

My hands shake while typing a message to
Mackenzie to let her know I'm back on my feet. My panic attack
earlier had spiraled wildly out of control, and I'm embarrassed I
needed the assistance of the team trainer. Every time I started to
calm down, Zeke would do or say something that sent my heart
rate sky high again. I'm pretty sure he almost kissed me. Twice.
I nearly melted at the way he looked at me in his suit jacket.

This was the first time in years I'd been alone with Zeke. I
agreed to his offer to drive home together (*Creator, help me,
how will I get out of that one?*) while drunk on Zeke's smile
and a rapidly escalating medical situation, but I'm regretting it
now. Our relationship is blowing right past friendship and I am
scared out of my mind.

"Everything OK?" he asks when I re-join him in the trainer's
room.

"Yeah. Kenzie was just checking on me." I find my jersey and pull it back over my head.

He holds my purse until my hands are free to take it from him. "Are you feeling well enough to head out?"

I nod. "Let's do it."

I follow Zeke out to the players' parking lot. The frosty December air feels wonderful against my overheated skin. I glance down at my smartwatch as another message from Mackenzie comes in. She already blew up my phone for updates on my condition. Now she's transitioned to sending all manner of colorful questions and emojis about my time alone with Zeke.

I notice it's silent and look up to see Zeke holding his passenger door open for me with friendly expectation. Silently cursing my sister, I drop my wrist and hope he didn't notice the large eggplant emoji that just appeared on my watch screen. "Sorry. Thank you."

His eyes dance as he fights to prevent his warm smile from turning into a cheeky grin. He absolutely saw the eggplant.

Zeke bids a goodnight to the security and pulls out into the busy streets of downtown Buffalo. I sit awkwardly in silence for the first few minutes, scanning my brain for a conversation topic. *How am I so bad at this?*

"Great game tonight," I finally say.

"Thanks." He flips his blinker on, merging onto the New York State Thruway.

Throw the man a freaking bone, Genesee.

"That was an incredible goal you scored in the third," I continue, "when you muscled that defender over and hit the behind-the-back shot." My cheeks flush at the memory. "It was really..." *HOT.* "...impressive."

Zeke's eyes dart over to mine, a genuine smile creeping over his face. "That was fun as hell, honestly."

That play made me weak in the knees. "You throw guys around a lot more than the last time I saw you play." *Me next, please.*

He chuckles. "That's why I've spent so much time in the gym the past few years. Defenders are getting bigger, and I wanted to keep up."

Silence falls back between us. I shoot Mackenzie a text to let her know I'll be home in about 30 minutes.

"What happened tonight?"

He asks the question I've been dreading answering. *Should I make up an excuse, or confront him with the truth?* The last time I was honest ended with corn flying.

"Being able to trust him is something only he can show you. And he needs to know that," Mackenzie had told me yesterday. She was right. I couldn't deny my feelings for Zeke any longer, and it was time to seize the moment.

I take a deep breath. "I had a panic attack."

His eyes dart from the road. He reaches over and gently squeezes my knee. "What's going on?"

My heartbeat thunders as I grab his hand with both of mine, trying to regulate my nervous system. "I was afraid you'd only invited me tonight out of obligation, and that you'd be disappointed to see me with your family." I pause. "You used to look right through me when you'd come home from college. I was scared that it would happen again."

My words hang in the air between us. It's terrifying to know my emotions are out there for him to see. The car is soundless, and I fear he can hear the blood rushing through my veins.

Zeke swears quietly to himself. He grips my hand tightly.

"Give me a minute," he finally says, his jaw ticking. "Please."

I nod, looking down at his hand in mine.

He pulls over into the first rest stop we come to, parking haphazardly under a streetlight. He unbuckles his seatbelt and turns to face me. His eyes are tormented. He leans forward to cradle my face in his hands.

"I wish we were somewhere I could get on my knees and beg for your forgiveness, Gen," he implores, looking at me so intensely I can barely maintain eye contact. "I was so wrong for how I treated you, and I'll spend the rest of my life making it up to you. If you'll let me."

"You don't have to–"

"I need to. I betrayed your friendship, and I abandoned you."

We stare at each other, so much pain and regret swirling between us.

"I can forgive you," I whisper, "but I'm not sure I can trust you again."

His agonized expression leaves me uncertain if he is about to kiss me, yell at me, or cry.

He closes his eyes and I reach up for his hands on either side of my face. I pull one to my lips, kissing his fingers.

"I'd like to try, though."

He returns my gaze, his eyes dark and mournful.

"It's more than I deserve," he rasps.

My watch buzzes again.

"We should get going," I say softly, reluctant to let him go.

He nods and settles back into his seat.

The remaining drive back to Cattaraugus passes quickly. My stomach tightens as we approach my house. I'm uncertain if it's from dreading the awkwardness of saying goodbye or disappointment that the night is ending. The truck's headlights light up my driveway as we pull in.

"Let me walk you to your door." Zeke puts the vehicle in park and starts unbuckling his seatbelt.

"That's not necessary," I reply, unbuckling myself and reaching for my purse.

He's suddenly on the other side of the passenger window in the time it takes me to get myself adjusted and reach for the door handle. He opens the door for me and smiles down as I look at him with exasperation.

"I've learned you're fast," he says, stepping back to let me out, "so I need to be faster."

We walk to the front door while I dig for my keys. This feels like the end of a first date, and my fingers are clumsy with nerves.

"Thanks for inviting me to–"

"I'm really glad you could–"

We both stop short, smiling as we stumble over each other's words.

"Sorry," I chuckle. "I appreciate the invitation tonight. I had a lot of fun."

He looks down at me and my stomach flip flops.

"I'm really glad you came," he says quietly. "I've missed seeing you at my games."

I draw in a shaky breath, uncertain of how to reply.

He shifts his weight to the other foot, hands in his pockets. "I've missed *you*," he rumbles, and I'm aware of how close we are together in the front alcove. Had I stepped closer to him, or had he?

"Zeke, I–" I wet my lips and notice his eyes drop to them briefly. His glance slowly crawls back up to mine.

My panic kicks in, and I find myself stepping into him for an awkward hug instead.

"I've missed you, too. Thanks again for–"

His arms tighten around my back, and I feel the gentle brush of his lips against my cheek. I pull back, dropping my keys in the process, and our gazes meet. My traitorous eyes are wide and wanting.

We'd never kissed as teenagers. Creator knows I'd wanted to, but Zeke was always a gentleman. A few kisses on the cheek were the closest we'd come. I'd spent countless nights dreaming of how it would feel to finally have his lips against mine, his hands in my hair as he held me close.

His hand draws me back to reality. He brushes the hair from my eyes and I exhale, my lids falling closed. I know I should walk away, but my feet feel like cinder blocks. *Fuck it.* I overthink every decision in my life, and I'm over it.

He softly cups my cheek. My eyes flutter open to find his ablaze, searching mine for permission. *Still a gentleman, I see.* I nod nearly imperceptibly and his grip tightens on my waist in response.

Just then, a huffing Mackenzie pulls open the front door. "Girl, just knock if you can't find your key–oh, shit."

I attempt to quickly step back out of Zeke's arms, but it's like fighting against quicksand as he holds me in place.

"I'm *so sorry*. Just...I'll...see you soon!" Mackenzie slams the door closed.

I chuckle nervously and attempt to squirm out of Zeke's grip again, but he will not budge. "I should probably–"

He brings a second hand up to frame my face before his mouth comes crashing down onto mine. I squeak in surprise as he steps us both backward until my back is flat against the wall of the house.

Zeke kisses me slowly and deeply, eliciting a moan from me as my hands run up his chest and wind around his neck. I'm engulfed by the delicious, clean scent of him and the thick softness of his hair between my fingertips. My knees tremble at the urgency of his kiss as he pins me against the siding. He must notice, because he brings an arm down to wrap firmly around my waist.

I feel like I'm being devoured. I'm aching and burning up from the inside out.

I'm vaguely aware of the sounds of a car driving by and it pulls us out of the spell we're under. We're both out of breath as he places his forehead against mine.

"Was that OK?" he asks hesitantly, trying to catch my gaze.

My breathing is labored, and I swear he must be able to hear my heart pounding against my ribs. "Oh, fuck yes."

He smiles and chuckles against my lips, bringing his mouth back down for another one, two, three kisses. I'm clinging to his open shirt collar like a life raft.

"We should have done this a long time ago," I mumble, my hands snaking up into his dark hair.

"Yes, we should've." He kisses me long and slow before pulling back slightly. "I'm so sorry, Gen," he whispers. "I'm so, so sorry."

I'm torn between blinking away tears and kissing him again to make him stop talking. All I want is to make out on my front stoop like a teenager. Maybe it's the mix of his shampoo and cologne making me dizzy, but I've given up fighting. I've been fighting my broken heart and resentment of him for so long, and I'm tired.

"I know," I whisper back, twirling his wavy tendrils between my fingers. "I believe you."

Zeke watches me intently, sadness and hope dancing between his eyes. "Can we start over? Reset the shot clock?" He smiles tentatively.

I nod and place my cheek against his chest. "I'd like that."

We stay wrapped up in each other for a while. "I don't want to leave you," he admits, kissing the top of my head.

"Well, I'm certainly not going to invite you inside on the first date," I tease, secretly hoping he calls my bluff. Mackenzie be damned.

His quiet laugh reverberates in his chest against my cheek, and he tips my face up to his with his index finger. "I wouldn't dream of asking." He kisses me gently before sighing and wrapping his arms back around me. "Actually, I will absolutely dream of that, if I'm being honest."

My insides tingle. The temptation to drag him inside is strong, and if he stays here for much longer I can't trust myself not to give in. I steel myself to come back to reality. "I should probably wish you good night."

I stand on my tiptoes to give him one last kiss. He groans and I'm back against the house again, swallowed up by his mouth and his hands deep in my tousled hair.

Grandmother Moon, I want this man to pick me up like a sack of corn flour and throw me into bed.

"Zeke," I manage to say against his incessant lips. "If we don't, mmmm. If we–" I might need to give up on full sentences for a while.

Eventually he comes up for air, pulling back from me with desire heavy in his gaze. "Look at how beautiful you are," he murmurs, brushing his thumb against my lower lip.

I am never going to let him go home at this rate.

The last thing I wanted was to stop, but I was increasingly aware of making a scene out in the open like this. "If we don't stop, Kenzie's going to send a search party," I quip.

He sighs and cradles my face between his hands. "I should let you go, shouldn't I?" He kisses me gently. "Can I see you tomorrow?" he asks hopefully.

If I wasn't mistaken, Zeke Jacobs was putty in my hands, and I couldn't resist the opportunity to toy with him. "Maybe."

His eyes narrow. "Maybe?"

I try to duck out of his hands but he cages me in with both his arms on either side of my head. I push against them but they don't budge. I'm going to need to lift heavier at the gym. "Yeah, maybe. I'll need to see what's on my schedule." I press my lips together tightly to suppress the grin threatening to break free.

He smirks. "OK. I deserve that." He tucks a piece of hair behind my ear and smiles when my eyes darken. I always knew we had good chemistry, but seeing it spark to life as adults was electric. "I'll call you?"

I nod and he kisses my hand.

By the time I stumble through my front door, I'm stunned, tousled, and itchy from where Zeke's stubble rubbed against me. I drop my purse and come face to face with Mackenzie, who's looking me over with arms crossed.

"I was about to send the Tribal Marshals to go looking for you."

I cough and bite my lip, a wide smile beginning to bloom.

"He kissed you." It was a statement rather than a question.

I grin stupidly.

"Well, it's about damn time!" she squeals and grabs me with glee. "You should've seen the murderous look he gave me when I opened the door on you two. Tell. Me. *Everything*."

Chapter 23

Zeke

Dawn broke, and I awoke feeling absolutely invincible. I scored two goals last night, my team won, and I kissed Genny. I was untouchable.

Wes is coming over soon to watch game footage with me, and I need to grab groceries. I'm hoping Genny's available to hang out this evening.

I grab my phone off the nightstand. I should still have her number, but it's been years since I've checked. I scroll through my contacts list and am relieved to see her on it.

Genesee Skye.

I smile like a dope and eagerly tap to open a text message. My phone pulls up the history of our correspondence and my grin falls apart.

The last time we'd exchanged texts was the summer after my freshman year. It could hardly be called an exchange given how one-sided the history was. I scroll back in time, seeing countless instances of Genny messaging to see how I was, how my classes were, and how I liked Hopkins. She wrote to congratulate me on big goals I scored, and to send me funny memes and stories from home.

In response, I almost never replied, except with the occasional 'thanks,' or 'things are good.' My God, what a shithead I was to her.

I toss my phone onto the bed with a groan. I can't bear to send her a new message and dredge up all those old memories on her end.

Ten minutes later, I'm ready for a fresh approach. I shower and get dressed, putting on some faded jeans and a black henley shirt. I grab my wallet, phone, and car keys before heading out, waving to my mom through her kitchen window as I pull out of the driveway.

When I eventually arrive at Genny's, I have groceries filling my back seat and my passenger seat holds hot coffee from Tim Horton's. I rummage through my glove box until I find a pen so I can scrawl a note on a napkin:

Good morning sunshine. And Kenzie.

Z

P.S. Up for a movie later?

I place the napkin underneath one of the two cups in a cardboard holder and head towards the front door. My smile grows the closer I get, remembering how delicious it felt to press

Genny against the house and kiss the daylights out of her last night.

I'm contemplating the best place to leave the coffee when I hear quick footsteps slowing behind me.

"Well, hi," Genny pants, taking off her headphones. She's dressed for a winter run, holding a fleece jacket she'd shed after warming up. I can't help but allow my eyes to admire the fit of her leggings and the way her chest rose and fell with her breath.

"Hi," I reply, at a loss for words. "I, uh, brought Tim's for you and Kenzie."

"That's nice of you." She crosses the distance to me and stands on her tiptoes to brush a kiss across my cheek. Her five-foot-seven frame feels small beneath me, and it activates a primitive urge to swallow her up in my arms.

"I didn't think I'd see you," I ramble. "I was just going to drop these off."

She chuckles, grasping the collar of my shirt and pulling my mouth down to hers. "Are you stalking me?"

I hold the beverage carrier to the side with one hand so I can brace her against my chest, kissing her softly. "I wasn't planning on it. Unless you're into that sort of thing."

She laughs against my lips, kissing me while backing up and continuing to tug me forward with the neck of my shirt. "Come inside, stalker."

"Gladly."

Genny pulls me inside the house, her lips never leaving mine. She takes the drink carrier from my hand and quickly sets it down on the kitchen table. She returns and presses me back into the closed door.

I moan into her mouth, nipping at her lower lip as she buries her fingers in my hair.

"Where's Kenzie?" I ask between urgent kisses.

"Still sleeping." She runs her hands across my chest and shoulders, murmuring in appreciation.

I sneak a peek behind her and see living room furniture, so I nuzzle against her neck and whisper in her ear. "Hang on."

She yips in surprise as I lean down and scoop her into my arms. I carry her across the small kitchen and sit down on the couch.

"It's really hot when you pick me up like that," she mumbles, trailing kisses down my jaw.

I chuckle, adjusting her position in my lap. "You're easy to lift."

Decades of longing and denial are pouring out of us. The gentle touch I imagined I'd have with her was instead a need to consume her, a hunger to make up for all the years I'd wasted without her in my arms.

From beyond the fog of lust I hear something, and wrench my mouth from hers. "Is that–"

"Kenzie!" Genny rolls off and onto the couch next to me, gasping for air.

A door next to the living room opens and we both smile sheepishly as a sleepy Mackenzie shuffles out.

"Good morning—Zeke?" She blinks at me.

I wave and adjust how I'm sitting.

"Zeke brought Tim's," Genny chirps.

Mackenzie yawns. "Were you two just making out?"

I itch the back of my head while Genny coughs delicately.

Mackenzie wanders over to the table and picks up a cup of coffee. "Thanks, Zeke. Carry on." She peels back the plastic lid and disappears into her bedroom.

Genny falls back onto me, giggling.

"I guess we're getting the experience of being walked in on by our parents," I laugh.

She smiles up at me and my heart swells with a deep happiness I haven't felt in a very long time.

I bend down to kiss her. "I should let you get back to your day. I've got Wes coming over soon."

She wraps her arms around my neck to keep me there. "Can I see you later?"

"Yes, please." I kiss her forehead. "Do you want to go out or stay in?"

"If we stay in, we're just going to make out the whole time."

"So, two votes for staying in?"

Her delighted laughter awakens a younger part of myself I hadn't realized was still there.

Chapter 24

Genny

Kenzie: Zeke and Genny made out last night

Chels: WHAT?! Where?!

Kenzie: The front porch.

Chels: Oh my god

Me: KENZIE!

Kenzie: You were taking too long to tell her, so I had to

Chels: Genny, what happened? More importantly, HOW WAS IT?

Kenzie: So good he brought her coffee before 8am on a Saturday

Chels: Damn girl. You're getting morning after pancakes next

Me: CHELSEA

Our group chat has blown up by the time I get out of my post-run shower. I settle in with my coffee and start recording an audio message for the girls. The past 24 hours has me wanting to kick my feet and giggle like a college girl.

Seeing Zeke at my door this morning was such a confidence boost. I'd spent my entire run reflecting on our kiss, trying to keep myself from spiraling into anxiety that it was just a fluke. You would think the fact that he tried to kiss me on three separate occasions would have brought me some comfort, but it was hard to unlearn old patterns of thinking. I absolutely attacked the man after seeing him. It was a fantastic way to start my day.

My phone buzzes while I'm braiding my wet hair on my bed.

Kenzie: Are you going to need a chaperone for your date tonight?

Me: Absolutely not

Chels: Absolutely not

Kenzie: In all seriousness, you two aren't going to last much longer without ripping each other's clothes off. Are you ready for that?

My sister was right, much as I didn't want to admit it. I'd been thirty seconds away from straddling Zeke on the couch this morning before Mackenzie came out of her room. That wouldn't have lasted much longer before I begged him to carry me to my bedroom. We were both adults capable of making sound decisions about physical intimacy, but I was worried my hormones were clouding my brain. I didn't want to regret moving too quickly with him given our history. The only thing worse than Zeke breaking my heart again would be if he broke my heart again after I knew what it was like to have all of him.

I sigh and pick my phone back up.

Me: I don't know yet. Probably not

Chels: Don't rush it. There are so many times I wish I would have waited

Chels: On the other hand, I bet Zeke's amazing in bed. He's very giving

Kenzie: He always puts others first

Me: Oh my god you two

Chels: I'm too single for this conversation

Chapter 25

Zeke

We're playing on the road this week, and Coach Travis works us hard at practice. We're playing the best team in the league tomorrow, the Calgary Stampede, and we've got a lot of cleaning up to do with our power play. Playing with the man advantage should make things easier, but we've struggled to convert those opportunities into needed goals.

Wes got called up from the Practice Roster to help us. We need someone to coordinate our power play attack while still providing some much needed defensive backup. I was hoping he would stay with the starters from this point forward, because he was working his tail off, but time would tell.

We head back to the hotel for showers, cleaning up a bit before going out as a team for dinner. I have Wes as my roommate for the first time since training camp. He pops up over my shoulder to wave goodnight to Genny while I video chat with her before heading out.

"I'm so glad you got your head out of your ass and made things right with her," he teases while hitting the elevator call button.

I laugh. "Yeah, well, it took me long enough." I see Sawyer and Jamie walking down the hallway from their room and wave them over to us.

"I'm glad you took the second chance," Wes says as the elevator dings its arrival.

"You two running on Indian time?" I quip, calling to my teammates.

"Wouldn't want to disappoint the ancestors." Jamie grins as he hustles to reach the doors before they close.

"I run on Indian time and I'm not even Native." Sawyer laughs.

"Yeah, but you've got honorary status as a friend of the program." Jamie winks. "Glad to have you back, Wes. We really need your expertise."

"Happy to help," Wes says.

"How's Ms. Genesee Beer?" Sawyer asks me with a grin.

"She hates that, you know," I reply with a chuckle.

"I figured. I didn't seem like her type." Sawyer jostles me, "Unlike someone else I know."

"Is this the woman you had in the locker room last week after the game?" Jamie asks.

Sawyer starts to make a crude comment, and I put my elbow in his solar plexus.

"Yeah. My friend Genny," I respond, ignoring Sawyer's wheeze.

"Girlfriend," Wes corrects me, holding the elevator door open once we arrive on the ground floor.

I scratch the back of my head. "I'm not sure if she's my girlfriend."

"You just called to say goodnight to her, bro," Wes teases, "and texted her when the plane landed in Calgary."

"That does seem a little more serious than a friend," Jamie deadpans.

"It sounds like you un-complicated things with her, then?" Sawyer grins. "I'm proud of you."

"She should come out with us after the next home game," Jamie offers.

We're meeting at a restaurant a couple of blocks away from the hotel. I put my hands in my coat pockets as we approach. It is freaking freezing outside here. "I'll invite her out *if* you guys behave." I point at Sawyer, who raises his hands in feigned innocence. "Don't hit on my girlfriend again, man."

He laughs, pulling open the entrance door. "I promise."

Chapter 26

Nisgówakneh

January

Genny

"**Y**ou should pack an overnight bag," Mackenzie insists. She watches me zoom around the house, changing outfits and looking for earrings.

"I'm not staying overnight," I reply, combing my fingers through my hair in front of a small mirror.

She raises an eyebrow. "The man is cooking you dinner at his apartment on his bye week. That's an invitation to spend the night."

I try on a pair of dentalium shell earrings, turning my head back and forth to assess if I want to wear them.

"Well, I'm not planning on spending the night," I reiterate. I frown and pull out the earrings.

It's mid-January, and Zeke and I have been spending every available moment together for the past month. I'd been to two more Outlaws games and gone out for drinks with his teammates afterwards. We had dinner with my family on Christmas Eve, and opened presents with his mom on Christmas day. We went sledding with my cousins after a big snowstorm and shared hot chocolate out of a thermos. He was there to greet me after long days at work and always quickly returned my messages. He has been attentive, patient, and communicative. So far, everything between us has been pretty close to perfect, which worries the hell out of me.

If everything is great, then why am I still waiting for the other shoe to drop?

"You don't have to *plan* on it," Mackenzie pushes. "Think of it more as an In Case of Emergency bag."

I huff and go in search of different earrings. "Fine. I'll stick an extra toothbrush in my purse. Are you happy?"

"Tuck a spare pair of underwear in there, too, and thank me in the morning," she calls across the house.

I emerge in a completely different outfit with no earrings. "How do I look?" I ask anxiously, doing a little spin.

Mackenzie whistles and claps in approval. I'm wearing my old winter standby of black tights and combat boots, along with a cream knit sweater and a hunter green skirt.

"Are you going to be warm enough?" she asks.

"Zeke will keep me warm," I grin.

"That's the spirit!"

A knock sounds at the door, and I panic. "Crap. I still need earrings."

Mackenzie gets up to answer. "Go get the green feather pair from my room and I'll stall Zeke."

I beam and make a beeline for Mackenzie's bedroom. Those are my favorite pair of her earrings. Chelsea made them a few years ago, and I keep forgetting to ask if she can make me a duplicate. I thread the hooks through my earlobes and give my hair one last fluff.

Zeke is laughing with Mackenzie when I emerge. He looks towards me and stops mid-sentence, his gaze moving up the full length of my body in appreciation. My insides flutter wildly.

"You look—wow." His eyes drink me in.

I take his hand and raise up on my toes to kiss his cheek. "Thank you."

He holds me in place with a hand on my lower back. "You're stunning," he murmurs in my ear, and goosebumps erupt down my arms.

He smiles at me, and I forget we have an audience until Mackenzie speaks.

"Well, have fun, kids!" she chirps, retrieving my purse from the couch. "I won't wait up!"

Zeke chuckles and holds my coat for me as I slip it on. "Thanks, Mom. I'll make sure she gets home safe and sound."

He helps me into his truck before getting in the driver's seat. His right hand slides over to the inside of my knee as he backs out of the driveway.

"Your legs are..." He whistles quietly, looking over at me with a shake of his head.

I giggle, unable to help myself. "Are you hitting on me, Zeke Jacobs?"

"I sure am," he sighs, turning onto the main road.

The short drive to Zeke's place feels like an eternity with his thumb rubbing against my inner thigh. His hand slowly inches higher on my leg.

"Zeke," I whisper, adjusting in my seat.

"Sorry," he apologizes, moving his hand back down to my knee. "I got distracted."

"I didn't tell you to stop."

"Jesus, Gen," he swears, gripping my knee with a squeeze.

We park and I turn into a feral animal. I unbuckle and grab the lapels of his coat as I tug his mouth onto mine. He moans and tangles his hands in my hair, holding me in place while he kisses me deeply. His tongue parts my lips and heat spreads through my body.

We're breathing heavily when we finally pull apart.

"Were we supposed to be eating dinner?" I pant.

"That was the plan." He kisses me again, gently taking my lower lip between his teeth.

I moan his name, feeling my remaining impulse control draining away. "We should...not do this in your mom's driveway."

"You're right." He tilts my head with his hand, kissing down the side of my neck. "We shouldn't." He nips my earlobe before wrenching himself away with a groan.

My head falls back against the passenger seat with a soft thump as I exhale erratically. So far, my insistence on not spending the night with Zeke was not looking like a successful gamble.

We manage to detangle from each other and prepare dinner. Afterwards, we wash dishes and clean the kitchen together. Zeke pulls out two wine glasses from the cabinet and hands them to me.

"I thought we could hang out by the fire for a while," he says, "as long as you won't be too cold."

I love the idea of cozying up with him outside. "That sounds great." I smile and grab a bottle of red wine from the counter.

We set up on the old porch swing, now tucked behind his garage apartment. Zeke gets to work starting a fire in the pit while I open the wine and spread out some fleece blankets. I kick my boots off and tuck myself under one of them, sneaking a photo with my phone once the flames kick into high gear. I send it to the girls' group chat along with a heart emoji.

Chels: Bow chicka bow wow

Kenzie: I told you to pack an overnight bag!

Me: We're just having drinks. I'll be home soon.

Kenzie: I hope you're not

Chels: I'm living vicariously through you. Get some!

I toss my phone to the other side of the swing as Zeke joins me. He hands me a glass of wine and we clink glasses together. I burrow into his chest, feeling utterly content.

We sit under the stars and tell each other stories. It reminds me of the days we'd lay on our backs in the field and talk about our dreams. I walk him through my college years getting a teaching degree from Buffalo State University, and tell him how much I love teaching at our old elementary school.

"It almost didn't happen, though, if I'm being honest," I admit.

He frowns. "What do you mean?"

I take a sip of wine. "My first student teaching placement was a disaster. The supervising teacher wouldn't let me take over any of the planning, and she badmouthed me to my observer."

A thundercloud descends over Zeke's expression as he listens.

"I overheard her tell another teacher that I was lazy and wouldn't be successful because I was Native." My jaw ticks angrily at the memory. "I felt so defeated and wanted to drop out of my teaching program."

"She said *what?*"

"I know. She's a horrible person." I sigh. "The only reason I stayed is because there was a Seneca girl in the class. She told me how much it meant to have a teacher look like her."

He kisses the top of my head. "I wonder what that girl grew up to become with you as her inspiration."

I smile. "I think of her often. I should see if I can find her."

"I'm sorry you had to experience that." He tightens his hold across my shoulder. "I should've been someone you could've talked to about it back then."

I squeeze his hand. "You're here now, and that's what matters."

Zeke pulls me in closer and tips my chin up for a kiss. The fire has died down, and the constellations have shifted across the sky. Our conversation flowed so easily that we lost track of time.

"It's getting late," he says softly. "Did you want me to drive you home soon?"

I rake my fingers underneath the bottom edge of his sweater, feeling the warm skin of his abdomen.

He brings his other hand over to cup my cheek. "You're also welcome to stay here, if you'd like."

"I'd like that," I reply, tracing my fingers from his hip to the middle of his chest. I press my palm against him, his heart beating fast beneath my touch.

He sweeps me into his lap, pulling my legs and the blanket across him. His kiss is dizzying, with one hand flat against my back and the other deep in my hair.

I lean against his upper body as I throw my legs over onto each side of him. He lets out a strangled moan when I sit down, straddling him as my skirt rides up.

"Gen–" I swallow his words, my kiss insistent. His hands come up to grip my hips, steadying me.

"Gen," he tries again, "I don't expect anything tonight."

"I know." I kiss along his jaw, the barest hint of stubble tickling my lips.

Zeke's hands sweep down my bare legs before drifting back up and underneath my sweater. "Can I bring you inside?"

"Let me just get my—oh!"

He stands and lifts me, carrying me in his arms like I'm made of air.

I never thought we'd be here again with each other. Would our story have a happy ending after all this time?

Chapter 27

Zeke

The girl of my dreams is in my bedroom and she can't keep her hands off me.

I lower Genny to her feet in front of my dresser. "You can sleep in something of mine if you'd like," I offer.

She tugs my lips down to hers, her hip bumping against a drawer handle. "I'll see what I can find," she mumbles against my mouth.

I reluctantly pull away. "Let me give you some privacy."

She pouts and I smile. "I'll be back in a few minutes," I assure her.

I splash cold water on my face at the bathroom sink, trying to pull myself back into full control of my body. I told her I didn't have any expectations for tonight, and I meant it. No matter what the heat speeding through my veins is trying to tell me. *I can exercise self restraint around her,* I tell myself. I change into sweats and a Hopkins Lacrosse t-shirt before exiting.

I stop dead in my tracks when I reach the kitchen.

Genny is on her tiptoes, trying to put back the wine glasses we'd used earlier. Her legs are bare and a black Outlaws t-shirt is creeping up her backside. Her long braid hangs over my last name and number on the back. It's the shirt I typically wear to autograph signings and other public events. Her athletic frame is swimming in it, and I feel a caveman urge to throw her over my shoulder and claim her as mine.

"Gen," I croak, rapidly losing the battle against a raging hard on.

"Hey!" she chirps happily. "I've just...about...got it." She pushes the last glass into place and closes the cabinet door, looking pleased with herself.

My eyes are unabashedly drinking in every inch of her from where I remain frozen.

"Sorry," she bites her lip sheepishly, "I tried on some of your shorts, but there was no chance of them staying on my waist. Is this too...not enough?"

I grimace, painfully hard. "No, it's...fine. You're good." I wrench my eyes away from her. "Maybe I should sleep on the couch? I don't mind."

Genny furrows her brow. "What? Why?" She walks towards me and I desperately start trying to recall random lacrosse statistics to distract myself from the way my shirt swells over the curves of her breasts.

"I think it might be..." I run my hand through my hair and exhale. "...challenging to sleep next to you. Like that."

She pauses. "Oh." Her eyes flick down to my sweatpants and she bites her lip again. The traitorous cotton fabric shows everything. She crosses the space between us and wraps her arms around my neck, pulling my mouth down to hers.

"What if we don't sleep?" she whispers against my lips.

"Are you sure?" I ask. I search her eyes and try to ignore the devil on my shoulder telling me not to think twice.

She kisses me gently. "Yes." Another kiss. "I'm very sure."

I groan and pull her hips close to me. "I don't want to rush anything." I truly didn't. The last thing I wanted was to mess up the progress we'd made after so many years apart.

She flattens her palm and runs it down my chest, eventually wrapping her fingers around the waistband of my sweats.

I hiss as she trails her index finger down the length of me. She hums in appreciation and traces her finger back up to my waistband.

"I need you," she whispers, looking up at me.

Fuck.

She catches her breath in surprise when I scoop her up, her bare legs dangling over my forearm.

"You are so gorgeous," I breathe onto her cheek. "I used to dream about you wearing my jersey, and everyone would know you were mine."

"Really?" she moans into my neck.

I kiss her as we clear the bedroom door. "I never could stop thinking about you."

I lay her down gently on the bed. She pulls me on top of her, hands entwined in my hair.

"I *am* yours," she says, her eyes locked onto mine. "I always have been."

<h1 style="text-align:center">Chapter 28</h1>

Genny

It's been a long time since I've been intimate with anyone, and this is *Zeke*. Had I thought about what it would be like to sleep with him? Abso-freaking-lutely. But the reality of it is terrifyingly awesome.

My legs fall open to accommodate him, his hardness pressing against me through his sweats.

"You have got to get some of these clothes off," I scoff, tugging on the back of his shirt. "It's not fair. I'm half naked and you're not."

"That's true." He pulls back to his knees and lifts his t-shirt over his head. He tosses it to the floor beside the bed. "Although I would argue that you were the one who decided not to wear pants."

He returns to me and I stop him with a firm hand to his chest. "Wait. *Wait.*"

Zeke freezes. "Everything OK?"

My eyes roam the expanse of his skin, overwhelmed by how much there is to look at. "Not if you don't let me admire this view."

He smiles as my hands reach up to run over his chest and shoulders. He's broad and chiseled, but with just enough softness to drive me wild. "This isn't good enough. Let me up."

He grabs my hand and pulls me up to a sitting position. "Better?"

"Not even a little bit. Come sit over here," I gesture, desperate to get my hands on him again.

He grins and scoots over until he's sitting with his back against the wooden headboard. "At your service."

He reaches for me and I straddle his lap. He moans into my mouth as I kiss him deeply. I take my time exploring every line and dip of his shoulder and chest muscles.

"Oh my God, Gen," he groans as I touch and kiss and lick every available surface of his torso.

I lean forward on his shoulders and grind against him. His teeth tug at my bottom lip when I begin to pant with need.

His fingers trace along my inner thigh and brush up against the edge of my panties. I press against his touch and he slowly lifts the fabric. I moan as his fingers slide over me.

"You're so wet for me," he groans, pressing his thumb against me.

I gasp as pleasure shoots through me.

His other hand tugs gently on my panties. "Lose these, please," he growls.

I quickly slide them down as he adjusts his position against the headboard. I straddle him again and he grabs my hips greedily, moving me back into position above his lap.

He pulls me close and whispers in my ear, "Do you want my fingers inside you?"

By this point, I'm aching painfully for him. "*Please*," I beg, my hips desperate against him.

We both moan loudly as he sinks a finger into me. "You feel so good," he exhales and his breath catches.

I'm lost in a fog of lust. I cry out his name when he adds a second finger, lifting and lowering myself onto them while his thumb maintains slow circles on my clit.

"I need you," I plead a few minutes later, practically in tears. Everything feels so intense.

Zeke smirks, his fingers keeping a consistent pace. "I want you to come first."

I whine in frustration. "I don't think I can. I never have before...during..."

He raises an eyebrow. "Is that a challenge?"

"No, it's the—*oh*!"

He changes the movement of his fingers and is now brushing against a spot that lights me up from the inside. *Holy shit.*

I've never been able to orgasm with a partner. A skill issue on the guy's part, possibly, but I get too deep in my head. I haven't been able to translate pleasurable sensations into the crest of a climax. No one's ever done *this* to me before, however.

I feel the first sparks of what I'm chasing and clench around his fingers.

"That's it." He wears a pleased smile. "Just relax. I've got you."

I'm seconds away from weeping, grinding against his hand. "Please. Don't stop."

I look up to find him watching me, his eyes heavy with desire. He reaches beneath my shirt and rolls my nipple between his fingers. A rush of sensation detonates within me.

"Come for me, Gen," his voice is husky and assertive.

I tumble over the edge into a rapidly cresting wave that goes on and on. My body is shaking from head to toe and I don't want it to end. I collapse onto his chest, my legs jello and my heart racing. He wraps his arms around me while my breathing stabilizes.

"That was the hottest fucking thing I've ever seen," he mumbles in my ear before softly kissing my jaw.

I nuzzle into his neck, still boneless. "How the heck did you do that?"

He chuckles. "I think you know how I did that."

I sit up. "No, for real. How?"

He shrugs and his hands wander under my shirt. "I just listened to your body." His thumbs brush across my nipples and I squirm. "I love seeing you in my jersey number, but we really need to get you out of this shirt," he says.

I tug on his waistband. "I could say the same about you and these pants."

Zeke grins. "Do you still want me?"

I scoff. "Do I still want you? Don't be ridiculous." I scoot back and start pulling down his sweats. He springs free from his boxers and I sharply intake my breath.

He kicks his pants off. "Why don't you get back on top? That way, you can make sure you're comfortable."

I can't take my eyes off him as he reaches into his nightstand.

"Condoms at the ready?" I arch my eyebrow at him.

He smiles sheepishly. "I didn't expect to use them. But I figured it wouldn't hurt to be prepared."

"Mmm hmm." I crawl over and straddle him again. I peel off my shirt and it's his turn to stare as my breasts tumble out.

"You are so beautiful," he says softly. "Your body is perfect."

"You're not so bad yourself."

He chuckles and grips my hips. "You sure you're ready?"

I kiss him firmly as I hover over him. "Will you be quiet and let me ride you, please?"

He moans and releases his hold on me.

Chapter 29

Zeke

My God. Genny is everything I dreamed of and then some.

I nearly lost myself watching her get off on riding my fingers. Now that I've had a taste of what she likes I want to master my craft.

She gasps softly as I enter her.

"Oh, Zeke," she breathes, pausing to inhale.

"Are you ok?" I ask quickly. "Am I hurting you?"

"No, it's just–" She sinks down a little lower and raises back up before lowering again with a quiet moan. "You're kind of a lot to handle."

My concern for her overtakes the masculine urge to preen over dick size. "Take it as slow as you'd like. I'm not going anywhere."

She raises and lowers herself, taking more of me each time. She's moaning and digging her nails into my shoulders, and it's becoming increasingly more difficult for me to recall the players on the last Outlaws championship team.

I glance down at the two of us together. "Look at how well you take me," I murmur in her ear. She moans and sits down fully.

"You're not such a gentleman when you're talking dirty," she teases, grinding against me.

"Are you filing a complaint?" I grit my teeth for self control as she begins slowly bouncing up and down on me.

"Absolutely not." She's out of breath and moaning more loudly.

I reach down and rub her sensitive spot. She clenches around me and I know she's already close, sensitized from her first climax.

"Grind on me, Gen," I murmur in her ear, knowing she likes it. "I want to feel you come again."

She whines in complaint but doesn't stop. "What about you?"

"You have no idea how good this feels for me," I say. "I'm fighting for my life over here."

She laughs and kisses me, her bare torso pressed against mine. I think I could live the rest of my life and never feel as complete as I do at this moment.

I reach back down to help her along and she tumbles over the edge, burying her face in my shoulder as she finds her release.

She's struggling to catch her breath when I lift her off me.

"You need a break," I tease, rolling over and pinning her beneath me.

"Is there a mercy rule?" she gasps for air.

"Not a chance." I nudge her knees with mine and she opens them eagerly.

She wraps her legs around my hips and I sink into her with a moan. I hold her close to me, kissing her and whispering in her ear with each thrust.

"You are so beautiful. You were made for me. You're mine."

She tightens her legs around me and I'm gone.

She holds me to her chest after, and I tune into the steady drumbeat of her heart. She runs her fingers through my hair and kisses the top of my head.

"I'm yours," she whispers back.

Chapter 30

Genny

I wake to the sun peeking through the curtains. Zeke is wrapped around me, his arm slung around my midsection and his head buried in the curve of my neck. A wave of deep contentment washes over me. *Last night was real.*

The next time I open my eyes the sun is brighter and Zeke is softly kissing my shoulder. I hum sleepily and press myself back against him.

"Good morning, sunshine." His voice in my ear is raspy with sleep. I didn't think his whispered murmurs could get any hotter, but I was wrong.

"Good morning," I reply, tilting my head back in order to pull his lips to mine.

He kisses me gently. "I can't believe you're really mine."

"To be honest, neither can I."

He laughs and turns me over to face him. He pulls me tightly against his chest and threads one of my legs in between his. *Hot damn.*

My body ignites beneath his touch. "You can't possibly still have the energy to–"

He rolls me onto my back and kisses me deeply with one hand beneath my neck. I moan against his mouth as he cups my breast.

"Seems like you may have some energy, too." His hair is delightfully tousled as it falls into his playful eyes.

"I *was* sleeping."

Zeke ignores me and trails kisses from the swell of my breasts down to my abdomen. "Are you sore from last night?" he asks.

"A little," I breathe, squirming under his touch.

He kisses along the waistband of my panties. He hooks his thumb around one side while holding me in place with the other hand. "Would it be all right if I used my mouth on you?" He looks up and my stomach flips.

I nod hesitantly. This was another activity that has never resulted in much of a good time in the past.

He grins and kisses my lower abdomen. "Thank you."

"I should be the one thanking—oh!" I switch from puzzled to surprised as Zeke steps off the side of the bed. He grabs my upper thighs and pulls me along with him.

"Sorry." He smiles widely. "I got too excited." He peels my panties down over my hips and positions me at the edge of the bed.

I shake my head at him in disbelief. "You can't be real."

He kneels next to the bed and gently raises each of my legs to his shoulders. My thighs are already trembling at the intimacy of the position.

"I'm real and I'm all yours," he smiles and kisses up the inside of my thigh.

It became immediately clear that my previous experiences were pale imitations of how this could feel. He's holding my hips down with one hand because I'm squirming so much against his mouth.

"Baby, you have to let me do my job," he chuckles. His breath breezes over me and the change in sensation is exhilarating. I attempt to keep myself still and I find it to be an impossible task.

His tongue is tracing patterns over my clit and my eyes roll back. My moans become louder as my thighs clench more tightly together around him. "I'm sorry," I pant. "I don't want to suffocate you."

He groans against me. "Don't worry about it. I'd enter Sky World as a happy man."

I laugh between breathy sighs. My body relaxes as pleasure rolls through my core.

"You might want to be more quiet unless you want the whole rez to hear you."

"I can't help it," I whine, reaching above my head for the edge of a pillow. "It's your fault."

He chuckles again, and I feel his fingers press gently inside me, coaxing against my inner wall. I pull the pillow over my face and moan loudly into it, recognizing his finishing move from last night. Paired with his tongue, I'm rapidly accelerating towards an orgasm.

My entire body shakes. My thighs squeeze together while I scream and curse his name into the pillow. His breathing is heavy against me and the thought of this gorgeous man on his knees for me and loving it catapults me over the edge. *Holy shit.*

My vision blacks out with the intensity of my climax. I'm vaguely aware of Zeke sliding my body further onto the bed and laying down next to me. He kisses my cheek and nuzzles my neck.

"I think the ancestors definitely heard you, but probably not the rest of the rez," he teases.

I mumble an indistinguishable retort, and he kisses me languidly.

"Want some breakfast?" he asks, rubbing his thumb against my cheek.

I grumble another noise and attempt to nod, completely spent.

He chuckles. "I'll take that as a yes. Get some rest and I'll be back."

Chapter 31

Zeke

I pull on some sweatpants and head to the kitchen, a huge grin breaking across my face.

Knowing I'd satisfied Genny so thoroughly makes my ego grow two sizes. It was so damn fun experimenting with her body and learning what she liked. I had a raging hard on from going down on her and seeing her come unglued beneath me.

I hum while I start the coffeemaker and heat a griddle on the stove. It's Sunday morning and life is good.

I'm flipping pancakes when a friendly series of knocks ring out on my front door. I set down my coffee mug and pull the door open.

"Hey, Mom," I smile nervously, terribly aware of my rumpled condition and a half-comatose Genny sprawled on my bed inside.

"Mind if I bring some things inside?" My mom gestures to the cloth bags hanging from her hands.

"Of course. Come on in. I was just making breakfast." I swing the door open for her and grab a bag from her shaky grip. "Are you feeling OK?" I ask with concern.

"Oh, I'm fine," she responds with her back to me, unloading groceries onto my counter. "I was cleaning out my fridge and found some food I won't get to before it goes bad. I figured you would be more likely to use them in the next few days."

I reach around her and grab packages of chicken and ground beef. "Thanks. I really appreciate that." I open the fridge and start shoving items wherever there's space. "Do you want coffee or something to eat?"

She smiles warmly, folding her bags into little squares. "I'd take a cup of coffee, if you're offering."

"Absolutely." I stand up and go in search of a clean mug.

She accepts a steaming cup a minute later. "*Nya:wëh*," she thanks me and takes a sip, humming her appreciation. "How was your date with Genny last night?"

I raise my mug for a sip to hide my big, stupid grin. "It was good. She's..." I sigh. "She's great."

She leans over and squeezes my hand where I'm leaning near the stove. "I'm so glad you two reconnected." Her eye catches on the pile of pancakes plated next to my elbow. *Uh oh.*

In slow motion, I see her glance over at my bare chest, which wouldn't be all that unusual for me, but then her gaze travels to where Genny's coat is draped over a kitchen chair. *Busted.*

My mom looks back at me and I cover a sheepish smile with a coughing fit. I'm an adult, but it still feels like being caught making out under the bleachers at Homecoming.

"She forgot that here last night." I itch the back of my head.

"Mmm hmm." She eyes me while sipping coffee. "Be careful with her, Zeke. Genny's like family to us, perhaps more than you realize."

My brows furrow in confusion, but she continues.

"She's been through a lot with you. With us." She looks at me intently. "I'd hate to see her heart broken again."

I swear internally. I'll be forever angry with myself for isolating myself from Genny.

"I know," I say quietly. "I don't want to lose her again, Mom."

She sets her cup down and reaches over for a hug. I squeeze her tightly and notice she feels thinner than usual.

"Are you sure you're feeling all right? You seem a little off." I pull back and search her face.

Her smile seems tight. "Yeah. I'm just tired, that's all." She clasps my hand. "Now, go have your breakfast and I'm sure I'll see you later."

Chapter 32

Genny

Kenzie: Genny didn't come home last night. No text. I'm hurt

Chels: So she's either loved up in bed with Zeke or dead in a ditch

Kenzie: Or enjoying those morning after pancakes

Chels: Oh yes! I forgot about those.

Me: I can see you two, you know

Kenzie: You're alive!

Me: Sorry. I haven't checked my messages since last night.

Chels: …

Kenzie: I can't believe you didn't give us live updates. Have I taught you nothing as your big sister?

Chels: OK SO…HOW WAS IT??

Kenzie: Tell me we accurately predicted Zeke's generosity

Me: You did

Chels: Way to go, Zeke! We had faith in you!

Me: 3 times

Kenzie: THREE?!

Chels: Like…1, 2, THREE?!

Me: THREE!

Chels: I continue to be too single for our conversations

Once Zeke left I took a few minutes to recover my senses and message the girls before jumping in the shower. Wrapped in a towel, I go in search of a shirt to wear while I dry off. *Mackenzie was right about that damn overnight bag.* I rummage through his drawers and my eyes fall on top of the dresser.

I pick up an old photo of us laughing in a field. Zeke is looking at me like I'm the sun, moon, and stars. A rush of emotion floods through me. I hadn't seen that look for a very, very long time. Now here we are again, and it feels like coming home.

I'm braiding my wet hair and wearing one of Zeke's high school lacrosse t-shirts when he returns with two cups of coffee.

"Hey, gorgeous." He smiles broadly, his eyes skimming over me and pausing on my bare legs. I delight in the knowledge that I turn him on so much.

"Hey." I smile back, accepting a steaming mug and a kiss.

"I've got pancakes in the other room when you're ready," he says.

"You're amazing." I close my eyes and take a warm sip. "Mmm, this is great. Thank you."

He sits next to me on the bed. "How are you feeling?"

I blush and take another sip to hide it. "I mean...pretty amazing."

He chuckles, placing a hand on my bare thigh. "Last night was incredible. *You* are incredible."

"Just last night?" I tease, inching closer to him. "Not this morning?"

"I mean, it was a real hardship. I can't believe you made me ravish you *again*."

I giggle and cover my face with my hand.

He pulls my palm to his lips for a soft kiss. "Are you feeling good about us?"

I smile. "Very much so. When can we do that again?"

"How much time do you have this morning?"

"Well, we don't want the pancakes to get cold."

Zeke takes my coffee cup and sets it down on the nightstand. "Then get the hell over here." He grins and tackles me onto the mattress.

Chapter 33

Nis'ah
February

Zeke

I'm running late for family dinner, which is unlike me.

My brothers gather for dinner at my mom's house every Sunday. Ezra drives over from SUNY Geneseo when he can, bringing my mom the level of joy that she only finds when her full wolf pack is home. Genny has joined us twice, but today she's traveling back from a teaching conference in Albany.

These past two months that we've been together have been the happiest of my life. I had been slowly coming back to life since my return to living on Cattaraugus, but the addition of Genny has exploded my world into technicolor. I am so deeply grateful for this second chance with her.

I'm having a shitty day. I came home after an away game in Philadelphia, where we lost badly and I got injured on a cross-check into the boards. I was able to finish the game, but today my knee is swollen and tender. I limped back to my apartment from the airport and immediately fell asleep. I woke up at 5pm feeling disoriented and exhausted.

"Nice of you to join us, Zeke," Miles quips as I stumble into the house. He's pulling a tray of acorn squash out of the oven.

"Sorry. I passed out after I got home this afternoon." I pull my mom to me and drop a quick kiss on her head.

"How's your knee?" she asks with concern.

"It's sore," I admit. "I'm going to need to take it easy this week."

"Make sure you do that," she says pointedly, and I chuckle. I'm pretty sure I've never *taken it easy* a day in my life.

"*Nya:wëh sgë:nö*!" Jordan's greeting rings out cheerfully as he walks through the front door carrying a large pot. Corn soup, I would guess.

"*Nya:wëh* for picking up your grandmother, Jordy," my mom thanks him.

"No problem," he responds, depositing the pot on the stove.

My brothers and I work together to finish preparing the meal, letting my mother and grandmother sit at the table and talk. The grill pan sizzles as Miles flips burgers.

"Don't burn those again," I needle him.

He scoffs. "That happened *one* time!"

"Mmm, hockey pucks for dinner!" Jordan rubs his stomach and Miles kicks him in the shins.

I glance at the table and notice my mom looks tired. Her typically lively eyes are muted, and her healthy glow is dulled. I make a mental note to bring her to the health clinic this week. She hasn't seemed like herself recently.

We enjoy our food and my brothers are boisterous, as usual. Jordan and Miles update everyone on their entrepreneurial progress, as they're working to start a small construction business on the rez. Ezra is in his last semester at Geneseo, and he's officially ready to be done with school.

"How are things with Genny, Zeke?" my grandmother asks kindly, her eyes twinkling.

"Fantastic," I reply with a grin.

"I cannot tell you how relieved we are that we don't have to avoid talking about her anymore, man," Miles states.

I frown. "You never had to do that."

"Let's just say you were a bit *touchy* about her for a long time."

I grumble, stabbing a piece of squash with my fork.

"Before you all scatter," my mom says once we're about to clean up, "I need to tell you something at the same time."

The sound of chairs shoving back from the table comes to a halt. My blood freezes as I look over at her, an uncomfortably familiar dread starting to trickle through me.

The four of us are silent as we scoot our chairs back into place and wait for her to talk. She grabs my grandmother's hand and squeezes it firmly.

My mom looks nervous. I feel the color draining from my face as she takes a couple of deep breaths.

"I want you to know that everything is going to be OK," she starts.

Thump. Thump. Time has slowed, and I can hear every beat of my heart.

My mom glances at me with a weak smile. "I've been feeling really run down for a few months, so I reached out to my doctor to figure out what's going on." She takes another breath. "I had some tests come back showing that I have non-Hodgkin's lymphoma."

The bottom falls out of my stomach. I close my eyes to steady the wave of dizziness that washes over me. *This can't be real.* We already lost my dad to cancer. I couldn't lose my mom, too.

"The good news is we caught it early, and it appears to be slow-moving," she continues, her voice sounding stronger. "My doctor says I can start with immunotherapy, and if it's effective enough I may not even need chemo or radiation."

My eyes are still closed, and I feel Jordan place a reassuring hand on my forearm.

"This is nothing like your dad's diagnosis," she says firmly. "We didn't know the signs and waited too long with him. It was an aggressive cancer that moved too quickly."

I slowly open my eyes and see my grandmother clutching my mom's hand, squeezing it intermittently for comfort.

"This time will be different," my mom states. "We know what we're up against. I have a good medical team up in Buffalo, and there's every reason to believe my treatment will be successful. I'm scared but I'm optimistic."

A chair shoves back and Miles gets up, wrapping my mom in a hug. "We're going to get you through this," he promises, looking at the rest of us. "We'll take care of everything so you can focus on fighting this."

She squeezes him, tears shining in her eyes.

Ezra comes over and joins their hug. A tear rolls down his cheek and I fiercely blink back my own. My baby brother was only eleven when our dad died. I couldn't bear to see him cry.

"It's different this time, Z," Jordan says to me under his breath, still holding onto my arm. "We're ten years older and wiser. We'll help each other through this."

My breath is ragged as fear seeps through me. I never wanted to be back here again. I feel like my world is falling apart and there's nothing I can do about it.

"Zeke."

I look up, and my mom is looking at me gravely, holding out her hand towards me. I grip it between both hands and summon a smile.

"I'll do whatever needs doing, Mom. Do you know your treatment dates? I'll rearrange my practice schedule so I can take you to them."

"I start next Monday. I'll need someone to bring me up to the cancer hospital in Buffalo each time, but I'm hoping we can rotate who that is."

"I'll just take you," I insist. "It's no big deal."

"It *is* a big deal." She squeezes me with a piercing look. "I have four adult sons and plenty of other loved ones. I don't want you shouldering everything yourself this time."

I frown as my brothers voice their agreement.

"We'll each take a turn or two," Miles says.

"I can come home on weekends and clean the house," Ezra offers. "One of us could prep dinners for the week."

"Please not Miles," Jordan quips. "My stomach can't handle it. *Hey!*" He bats away a balled up napkin thrown across the table.

"I'm literally available every Monday," I reiterate. "Let me take you to your appointments."

"Come here," my mom requests, holding out her arm for a hug.

I sigh and get to my feet, kneeling next to her chair and embracing her.

She holds me tightly. "I want things to be different this time," she whispers. "I need *all* of you."

Jordan piles onto us with an embrace. "We've got this, Mom. All four wolves have a role to play."

"OK," I agree reluctantly. "But if anything comes up make sure you let me know."

I don't know how we're going to get through this, but I'm going to try.

Chapter 34

Genny

What on earth is going on with Zeke?

He's been difficult to get a hold of, which triggers my past anxiety. I haven't seen him since late last week, and his responsiveness to texts has been pitiful. It's not unusual for us to go several days without seeing each other, but we typically text or call in between. I thought about stopping by his apartment after dropping off Delores' groceries, but I didn't want to entertain my paranoia. If something was wrong, he would tell me. I felt confident about that.

"*Hae'* Dee Dee," I call out in greeting as I muscle through her door with grocery bags.

"*Nya:wëh*, Genny." Delores comes around the corner with a tired smile.

My Spidey senses spring to life. I look over at her as I'm unloading items into the fridge. "How are you feeling?"

She pulls out a chair and sits with a quiet sigh. "It's been a challenging week."

"I'm sorry to hear that," I say. "What's going on?"

She lifts her head, looking surprised. "Have you spoken to Zeke?"

The Spidey senses were turning into flashing red sirens. "Not really. He hasn't been around much this week, it seems."

Delores mutters something that sounds suspiciously like "*that damn boy.*"

"Come sit with me," she instructs, gesturing to the chair next to hers.

My insides are quivering by the time I make it to the table. My heart is in my throat.

She takes my hands in hers. "Elaine received a cancer diagnosis last week."

My mouth pops open in shock and horror.

"Her prognosis is positive, and she starts treatment next week," Delores continues. "I'm worried, because of course I am, but Elaine is being very brave and optimistic."

I close my eyes and breathe deeply. "Does Zeke know?"

She nods. "Elaine told the boys on Sunday."

A pit settles into my stomach.

"I think Zeke is having a hard time with it," she observes gently, "and it wouldn't surprise me if he's isolating himself right now."

I nod slowly, afraid to let my mind go too far down the road of possibilities.

"I'll talk to him," I tell her, "and I'll get the community mobilized to help Elaine over the next few months."

Delores smiles in gratitude. "*Nya:wëh*, Genny. Elaine wants to do things differently this time. We don't have to repeat the experience with David."

I see the haunted look in her eyes and squeeze her hands. "It'll be different. I promise."

I finish putting the groceries away and leave Delores with a long hug. I pull out my phone and call Zeke before I've gotten into my car. I'm relieved when he answers.

"Hey," I say, starting my engine. "I'm just leaving your grandmother's house."

"Oh. Right." He sounds disoriented. "I forgot it was Thursday."

"Are you heading to Buffalo soon?" I ask, backing out of the driveway. He should have practice tonight, since there's a home game tomorrow.

"Yeah."

I'm worried. I get on the road and start driving towards his place.

"Is there enough time for me to stop by?" I ask. I'm showing up at his front door regardless of the answer.

"I guess so."

My stomach clenches as years of uncomfortable memories and emotions flood my system. *I can't do this again with him.* I push those thoughts to the back of my mind.

"OK. I'll see you in a couple minutes." I hang up before he responds and throw my phone into the passenger seat, choking back a sob.

It's going to be OK, I tell myself. We're older now. We've talked all this stuff through already. He just needs some comfort. He's still in shock.

I pull into his driveway, feeling decidedly ill. I take a deep breath, throw my shoulders back, and climb the stairs to his apartment.

Chapter 35

Zeke

My mom's diagnosis has completely upended my life.

I had never considered what it would be like to go through this again with another family member. The shock and pain of my dad's death had been too immense, and my brain couldn't allow itself to think it could happen a second time.

I'm grateful I needed to rest my knee this week, because there was no way I could have gotten myself to the gym after Sunday's news. I canceled training with Wes and retreated into my apartment. Genny had called and messaged every day and I'd tried to act normal. I suspect she saw right through me. I wasn't ready to tell her about my mom yet, because that would mean it was real.

My knee is still tender, and I think there's a good chance Coach Travis keeps me out of tomorrow's game. We've had a few offensive injuries lately, and as a result the Outlaws are in the middle of a three-game losing streak. Normally I would be doing everything I can to rehab and play through the pain, but I can't bring myself to feel much of anything about it.

I open the door at Genny's knock and she enters, her eyes ablaze with worry and concern. I don't have a chance to say anything before she slides her arms around my waist and pulls me tightly against her.

"Your grandmother told me about your mom," she says quietly, her cheek against my ribs.

I blow out an emotional breath, hesitantly wrapping my arms around her in return. This is a familiar position for us, and my heart beats painfully at the memories it brings up.

We continue to hold each other, and I wince when I shift my weight to the other foot.

She pulls back quickly. "Oh shit, your knee. I completely forgot. Let's sit down."

I walk painfully over to the couch with her. This injury is pissing me off.

"You shouldn't play this week," she asserts. She helps me sit and then raise my left leg onto the couch.

"I need to play," I grumble.

"Don't be a dumbass." She glares at me with a touch of irritation and I swallow my snarky response. "This is not the time to be a hero."

An uncomfortable silence falls between us.

"I'm sorry I didn't tell you about my mom," I finally say. "I just wanted to hide from everything."

Genny sits next to me. "I know you're not used to letting people in when you're struggling." She pauses. "Especially me."

I cringe. She's right.

She takes my hand and squeezes. "I don't have all the details about your mom's diagnosis and treatment, but I know this doesn't have to be a repeat of last time." She looks at me and I see the fear in her eyes. Fear of how I'm going to respond.

My mom and brothers had looked at me the same way on Sunday. *Am I such a headcase that everyone is scared to upset me?*

She watches me. "The community has a chance to organize this time. Your brothers are grown, and you have all kinds of support to help shoulder the burden of your mom's treatment needs. We didn't have the benefit of time with your dad's diagnosis."

I shake my head. "I think I should request time off from the team. Mom's going to need someone to bring her back and forth for treatments, and she's going to feel like shit in between sessions. I'm lucky to live next door and can be her primary caretaker."

Genny continues holding my hand, deep in thought. "I think we can get full coverage from the community to help your mom. You'd be part of that, of course," she reassures me, noticing my frown, "but not the only one."

"I don't know–"

"In my opinion, try to focus on your work with the Outlaws as much as possible. You need a distraction. Of course, you'll also be helping your mom. But you can't let it consume you." Her eyes are pleading. "We need you. *I* need you. And if you let this take over your life, then we lose you again," her voice trails off in a whisper.

My head falls back in frustration. My brain sees the logic of what she's saying, but doesn't want to engage with it.

Genny leans me back against the arm of the couch and crawls onto my chest, laying against me while avoiding my injured knee. She stays there for a while, and the weight of her brings some calm to my wild nerves. My arms come up around her and I breathe deeply into her hair. Her scent reminds me of home, family, and safety. She brushes a soft kiss against my lips and my body sparks to life.

I hold her close and kiss her more deeply. My hand cradles the back of her head and tangles in her dark hair. It was the first time I'd felt much of anything in four days.

She looks up at me and smiles. "There you are. I couldn't find you."

I shift my hips and re-position her on my lap. Her eyes flash with surprise and amusement when she feels me growing hard beneath her. "I need you, Gen," I whisper, desperate to keep my numbness at bay for a little longer.

"I need you, too," she echoes, circling her hips against me. "I've missed you."

I bite my lip to suppress a quiet moan.

She climbs off of me and sinks to the floor, tugging the waistband of my pants and shifting me forward. "Let me make you feel good," she insists, pulling me free from my boxers.

My mind goes blank once she takes me into her mouth, my body entirely focused on how damn good she feels. I comb my hands through her hair, holding it back and out of her face. She moans and takes me deeper, her hands gripping my thighs.

She's got me seeing stars, and I gently tug on her hair a few minutes later. "Let me get inside you," I implore, feeling the edge approaching.

She shakes her head and briefly pulls away from me. "Don't worry about me. I want to finish you like this."

I groan and she wraps her lips back around me. Her pace has increased and I'm rapidly losing control.

I fall off the cliff and she moans in satisfaction, holding me in her mouth until my body has quieted. She kisses the inside of my thigh and pulls my clothes back into place.

I kiss her when she comes to sit between my legs, my breathing heavy and my limbs tingling. "That was unbelievable. Thank you."

She nuzzles into my neck. "Thank you for letting me."

I chuckle with disbelief that this woman is mine. "I need to return the favor."

"You don't need to. I know you've got to get on the road soon."

"You seemed to enjoy yourself just now," I murmur into her ear, my hands roaming beneath her sweater. "I can't let you go home like this."

"You're barely even mobile," she points out, but doesn't protest when I flick open the button of her jeans and gently coax her back to be flush against my chest.

"I can work around that." I pull her zipper down with one hand and unhook her bra with the other.

She shudders and presses against me, lifting so I can push her pants over her hips. She kicks them off and I hold her in place between my thighs.

I moan loudly when I sink my fingers into her. "You're so wet from using your mouth on me."

She's already panting, thrusting against my hand and making me hard all over again. I kiss down her neck and her nipples stiffen in response. She squirms and I tighten my grip, keeping her pinned against my chest as I pleasure her.

I enjoy the hell out of bringing her to climax with my fingers while my other hand plays with her breasts. She's so loud when she tumbles over the edge that I put my hand over her mouth to quiet her.

"We're going to get the cops called on us," I tease, loving the vibration of her moans against my hand as her body shudders in my arms.

She collapses against me, thoroughly spent, and I wish we could stay like this forever. I trail kisses down her jaw and hold her until the last possible moment.

"You need to leave," she reminds me.

"I wish I didn't have to." I tuck her into my chest. "Can I see you after the game?"

"I'll be here waiting for you," she promises.

Maybe, just maybe, I'll get through these next few months if I have her by my side this time.

Chapter 36

Genny

I stop at Elaine's after leaving Zeke. I suspect the team will send him home because of his knee injury, and I want to get the ball rolling before he comes back. I think I've raised his spirits, but I still don't trust him to not screw everything up with his martyr complex.

Armed with research and a load of phone numbers from Elaine, I start pulling together a plan. Zeke's brothers are great, but they could use some help.

Jordan: You're the best, Genny

Miles: For real. An honorary wolf pack member

Jordan: Creepy. She's dating our brother

Miles: We'll leave it up to the clan mothers to legislate

Ezra: You guys are so weird. Thank you so much for helping us, Genny

Me: I'm happy to help. I organize children for a living so this isn't much different

Miles: *GIF of a hospital Burn Unit*

Ezra: Don't lump me in with those two clowns

Me: Never, Ezzie. Jordan, could you take her on Monday? The first infusion will last all day so she'll need extra support.

Jordan: I'm on it. As long as Zeke doesn't throw himself in front of my car to block me. Where IS Zeke by the way?

Me: I left him off the chat until he's back from his game

Miles: *GIF of an armadillo rolling into an armored ball*

Jordan: Hey how'd you find that gif of Zeke avoiding his problems?

I chuckle and take screenshots of my Amazon cart to share with the group.

Me: Reddit says she'll probably feel nauseous, cold, and bored while she's there. I'm building an Amazon order so let me know what else I should add.

Ezra: What about a pair of headphones so she can listen to music or audiobooks?

Me: That's a great idea.

Jordan: Peppermint candies? Hand warmers?

Me: Love both of those. Keep 'em coming!

The boys send me money to split the cost of the order and I submit it. Everything should arrive just before Elaine's first treatment.

It's way past my bedtime. I'm feeling tired but push through. I find a website that coordinates meal train sign ups and configure it for the Jacobs family. Elaine will be exhausted between treatments, so people can volunteer to bring meals each week. I text the link to every woman I know on Cattaraugus, and it's shared with just about everyone else almost instantly. Most of the meal slots are filled within an hour. *Matriarchal societies, we get shit done.*

Zeke texts the next morning to say his coach is holding him out of the game, thankfully. I knew he'd never rest unless the staff made him. I'll give him a chance to pick a treatment appointment or two to cover in the coming weeks, but I'm grateful Jordan can take her to the first one. It's likely to be the most stressful, and I trust him to be a steadying force.

"I need to hire you to run my life," Mackenzie states on our drive home from school on Friday. "I can't believe you pulled all of that together in just a few hours."

"Getting people organized is the easy part," I sigh.

"Zeke is going to be the hard part," she says with a sympathetic smile. "And for once, I don't mean that in a dirty way."

I nod. "You're absolutely right."

"Although if you keep him hard, it'll probably make things easier."

I throw an elbow at her as I turn my key in the front door.

Chapter 37

Zeke

I flop onto my bed and stare blankly at the ceiling. *What a shitty day.*

I just got home from my mom's second infusion. It did not go well. She reacted to the medication and needed to stop and start a few times. Her first treatment was even harder, and she wound up at the cancer center with Jordan for eight hours. It was agony to watch her struggle through the pain and exhaustion, no matter how much she tried to put on a brave face.

My phone buzzes and I sigh heavily. *What now?*

Wes: Hey man. How did things go this morning? I missed you at the gym

Me: Not great. It's been a rough day

Wes: Want to talk about it? I can come by

Me: Not really. Just trying to get through the rest of the day

Wes: Would it help to get out? Sawyer's in town visiting friends and crashing at my place tonight. We could go play darts somewhere

Me: Thanks for the offer. Genny's coming over after work so we'll probably just hang out here

Wes: Bring her along! It'd be fun

Me: I'm feeling wiped after earlier. I think I'll sit this one out

Sawyer Lane has been added to the chat

Wes: Sorry. I brought in reinforcements

Sawyer: Z, you have to come out with us tonight! I'll buy you a drink.

Me: I'm not feeling it tonight. Another time

Sawyer: Since when have I ever taken no for an answer? You're coming.

Wes: It would be good for you to get out of the apartment. At least see what Genny says

I set my phone down and pull a pillow over my face. I know my teammates are trying to help, but they're stressing me out.

The only things keeping me sane lately are sleep and sex, and both are thanks to Genny. She's been spending most nights with me, even though it's inconvenient for her commute with Mackenzie. She makes me dinner, blows my mind in bed, and then lays in my arms until I fall asleep. Every morning my stress levels reset, but by night's end she's calmed me enough to get some needed rest.

It would make for a pretty fucking incredible life if I wasn't stuck in a spin cycle of anxiety the other 75% of the day.

My front door creaks open and I breathe a sigh of relief. *She's here.*

I smile weakly at Genny as she enters my bedroom.

"Hey," she says. Her eyes assess the sight of me laying flat as a corpse in the middle of the day. She curls up next to me in bed and rests her head on my chest. "Do you want to talk about today?"

I shake my head and wrap her tightly in my arms. "Can we just lay together?"

"Absolutely."

My world stops spinning whenever I hold her. My pulse slows to match hers and my tense muscles relax. When Genny is with me I feel I can handle anything.

And I hate myself for it.

I hate how much I've come to depend on her. I hate that I'm a mess without her. I should be strong enough to lead my family through this tough time, but instead I'm the weak link. I'm barely getting through each day.

She deserves better than me.

The intrusive thought creeps in uninvited. I swallow painfully and try to chase it away.

"Let's go out tonight," Genny suggests. "You've barely left the apartment in weeks."

"I don't want to."

"I bet you'll feel differently once we go somewhere." She pauses. "Wes texted me."

I groan. "He's killing me."

She tips my face down to hers. "Come on, let's do it. I haven't played darts in forever, and it would feel good to forget about everything for a few hours." She kisses me softly. "What do you say?"

Her eyes dance with excitement and I don't have the heart to turn her down. "All right. But just for a little while."

She squeezes me and hops out of bed. "Let me run home and grab some cute clothes. It'll be like a date." She beams at me.

"A date with two other dudes?"

She laughs and kisses my forehead. "Don't rain on my parade. I'll pick you up in a couple hours."

"You made it!" Wes says with a smile as we walk into the sports bar later.

Genny gives him a long hug. "We're here! Thanks for the invite."

Sawyer hands her a frosty beer. "A Genny beer for Genny. I'm sorry I used a lame pickup line on you a while back." He grins and she laughs heartily.

"You're forgiven. And thank you." She takes a sip.

"What're you drinking, Z?" Sawyer asks as we approach the bar.

"Just a water for me," I respond.

Sawyer frowns. "I'll buy you something to eat, then."

"I'm not really hungry," I say. My appetite has been nonexistent.

Genny squeezes my hand. "You should eat something. You've had a long day."

"Maybe later."

The four of us pass time chatting and throwing darts in between drinks. Genny mops the floor with all of us, naturally, although Sawyer had a strong showing.

"How do you *do* that?" he asks incredulously as she hits another bullseye with a satisfying *thunk*.

"We can't all be Creator's favorite." She collects her darts from the board.

He throws his head back with laughter. "I like her," he says to me.

"Me too." I smile but it doesn't reach my eyes. I'm glad Genny's having a good time, but I'm desperate to crawl back into bed and hide from the world again.

Wes lines up his next shot. He misses the dartboard by a mile and swears under his breath as his dart clatters to the floor.

Genny nudges my shoulder and tucks herself under my arm. "You OK?" she asks.

I watch as Sawyer shows Wes how to improve his form. "Yeah. I'm fine."

"Hey." She tugs at my shirt and I look down. Her brow is furrowed above her dark eyes. "Do you want to head home?"

I exhale with relief. "Yes, I do."

"No problem. Let's wrap this up."

I feel like a zombie as we walk towards my truck. My brain is foggy and my body exhausted.

Genny clutches my arm. "I'm worried about you," she says.

I force a smile. "Don't be. I'm just tired after a busy day."

She squeezes my bicep. "I hope it's OK that we went out tonight."

"Yeah, of course." I brush a kiss against her soft cheek.

It's a lie. I can feel myself spinning into a dark place mentally and don't know how to stop.

Chapter 38

Oàgaida:töh

The path slants this way and that

Genny

The March sun is softening the snow pack and carving melted paths in the grass. Temperatures vary dramatically from day to day, as Mother Nature fights to be released from her hibernation. Much like the Earth, my life has become muddy and mercurial.

I rush out of the school as soon as my students are dismissed. I have math homework to grade and lessons to plan, but I'll need to do that tonight after Zeke falls asleep.

"Pow Wow Fitness tonight?" Mackenzie asks hopefully as we pile into our car.

I feel a pang of longing. "I wish I could go. I really miss it."

"Then come with me. Zeke can manage without you for an hour or two." Her warm eyes are downcast. "Life isn't the same without you around."

"I know." I fidget with the end of my braid. "It's been a lot. I'm hoping things will start settling down in another week or two."

I pray that I sound more confident than I feel, because I'm struggling. The frantic pace of the past month is wearing me down. I'm basically living with Zeke and have reordered my life to spend every free moment with him. Work is being done in the margins of my days, and exercise has taken a backseat. I've barely seen my family and have stepped away from helping in the community. Cut off from my usual routines, I'm hanging on for dear life.

I'm afraid that if I stop moving I'll lose him.

Zeke's pushing me away again. I see it in his distant eyes and half-hearted touch. We're together constantly, but I rarely see him come out from the shadow of his depression. I can tell he's fighting against the urge to isolate, but it's seeping in anyway. Elaine's difficulties during her early treatments have added to the weight he's carrying.

"Have fun at dance class, OK?" I say to Mackenzie as I prepare to exit the car. It's pouring and I'm grateful my sister brought my raincoat this morning.

"I won't, but I'll go anyway."

"Don't make me feel bad." I sigh. "Oh! Are you able to get Delores' groceries tonight?"

"Yeah. I'm going to the store now."

"Thank you." I lean over to hug her. "I really appreciate you covering for me."

"Anytime, little sis." She squeezes me.

I steel my nerves and thrust open the car door. I pull my hood down against the rain and sprint up the steps to Zeke's apartment.

The door slams behind me as I enter and shake off water. I plop my work bag onto a chair in the darkened kitchen. It's eerily quiet. It's not unusual these days to find Zeke in bed when I arrive mid-afternoon, but his room is empty when I check. *His phone is on the nightstand, so he can't have gone too far, right?*

I head back out into the deluge to check on Elaine. Water rushes down the roof and drips noisily in pools under the stairs. I'm halfway to his mom's house when I notice movement out of the corner of my eye.

The old porch swing sways gently in the wind. Zeke sits hunched over and he's absolutely drenched. My boots splash on the wet grass as I trek towards him.

"What are you doing out here?" I shout over the downpour.

He glances up and my stomach drops. His face is distraught.

"The weather matches my mood," he says simply.

"Why don't you come inside? You can shower and I'll make you some tea," I offer.

He shakes his head. "I can't."

"Why not?"

He pushes the swing back and forth. Several seconds tick by without a response.

I take a seat next to him and wrap my arms around his.

"Come inside," I repeat. "You must be freezing."

"You should go," he rasps. "You're getting soaked."

"I won't leave you."

Zeke hangs his head. Rivulets of water run down his hair and into his eyes.

"It feels right to sit in the rain."

"Then I'll sit here with you." I lace my fingers between his and rest my head on his shoulder.

I'm not sure how many minutes pass as we silently watch puddles form in the yard. My clothes are waterlogged and I begin to shiver.

"I don't deserve you," he whispers as the rain finally lightens.

"I'm exactly where I want to be," I assure him with a kiss.

He gathers my hands between his and blows on them. "We need to warm up." Relief floods my body at the spark of life behind his eyes.

I nod enthusiastically through chattering teeth.

We kick our squishy shoes off next to the front door and I eagerly shed my raincoat. Zeke takes my hand and tugs me towards the bathroom. He starts the shower while my numb hands fumble with the buttons on my slacks.

"Let me help you." Zeke's voice rumbles against my ear as he flicks open the clasp. He slowly peels my wet clothing off one item at a time and tosses it to the floor as the room fills with steam.

I pull his mouth to mine as he begins to gently unravel my hair from its braid.

"Are you feeling any warmer?" he asks between kisses, dragging his knuckles across my bare skin.

"Very much so," I answer, unbuttoning his jeans.

He pulls me into the shower once we're free of our clothes. He presses me firmly against the wall as the hot water beats down on us. I close my eyes and surrender to his touch, praying the warmth can also thaw a path through the darkness in his mind.

Zeke

It's Monday morning and I'm about to puke.

My mom's at her third infusion appointment, and I check my phone for updates from Miles. Today is a critical day for the future of her treatment. The doctors are hopeful her body is gradually adjusting to the cancer medication, but if she has another bad reaction at today's appointment they will likely discontinue the infusions as an option.

My workout has been absolute shit while I wait to hear how things are going: I'm not lifting as heavy, my cardio endurance is lower, and I keep taking breaks to pace around the gym.

"You're doing great, Z," Wes calls out from his weight bench. "It's a hard day but you showed up to put the work in."

I'm heading to Denver for an away game this weekend and I'm sick with worry about leaving. *What if something happens while I'm halfway across the continent?* Old habits die hard, and

I can't seem to break through my pattern of thinking that says I'm the only one who can do everything.

Lately, any hours I'm not spending in the gym or with Genny are with my mom. I'd finally convinced her to start watching *Reservation Dogs* with me instead of the 5,456th episode of The Price is Right. We laughed and joked about who on Cattaraugus was most like each of the show's ridiculous characters.

"Your father would've loved this," my mom said with a smile last week. "Especially Uncle Brownie."

I laughed. "He would've. He thought Natives were the funniest people in the world."

"Well, we are." Her eyes sparkled. I treasured these new memories we were making.

After the gym I head home. My plan is to lie around feeling anxious and check my messages until Genny comes over. My brain and body feel directionless.

I'm walking up the stairs to my apartment when my phone buzzes.

Miles: We're on our way home. We made it a couple of hours, but then Mom had trouble with the medication again so they stopped the infusion

Me: Fuck

Jordan: Does this mean she's looking at chemo instead?

Ezra: How is Mom feeling? Is she OK?

Miles: She's pretty sick right now. I put her seat back so she can rest in the car.

Miles: I'm not sure what's next. The doctors need to talk about where we go from here.

Me: Chemo would rip her apart. She's already so frail right now.

Ezra: I'm worried. When will the doctors know more?

Miles: Not sure yet. I've got to get on the road, but I'll update more once we get back.

I slam my front door behind me in rage and frustration. I wish I was still at the gym, because I really need to hit something. I kick a chair out from the table and collapse into it, my head falling forward into my hands.

I hadn't been doing great, but I had been hanging on. This update has knocked down the house of cards I'd been precariously balancing. I push back from the table and pace around my apartment, desperate to expend energy but uncertain of what to do.

There's a knock at the door. "Come in!" I bark, continuing to walk back and forth.

Jordan enters, watching me stomp around for a minute before he speaks.

"Come on, Z. Let's go for a walk."

"I don't want to."

"You're literally already walking."

I grumble and ignore him.

"You. Out. Now." He gestures towards the door with his head.

"I. Don't. Want. To."

"I'll fucking body check you out of here, man." He narrows his eyes at me.

Jordan's not a small guy, but I have a couple inches and 30 lbs on him. "You know you can't move me."

We stare at each other in annoyance for a while before I finally huff with exasperation.

"Fine. Let's go."

We silently wander down side streets with no destination in mind. A couple of rez dogs begin to follow us, so I throw sticks for them to chase. I find the repetitive movement therapeutic and it gives my nervous energy someplace to go.

"We need to get it together for Mom," Jordan eventually says.

"You think I don't know that?"

"I don't know that you do, because you're a fucking mess, Zeke."

I grind my teeth and chuck a stick so hard I wince. It would serve me right to pull something in my shoulder doing stupid shit.

He stops and faces me. "We're all struggling, but we need to keep it in check. Mom needs us, especially after what happened today." His jaw ticks.

"You don't know how hard it was last time with Dad," I spit. There's a deep anger rising in my body.

"Yes, I fucking do!" He runs a frustrated hand through his dark hair. "I don't understand why you act like you were the only one around when Dad died. I was fifteen, and the oldest one left while you were off at college."

"While I was improving my game so I could get drafted and bring in money for the family, you mean?" My voice is getting louder.

Jordan starts walking again and I follow, looking for a fight.

I push his shoulder from behind. He spins around and glares at me.

"What is your fucking deal, man?" he growls.

"You tell me, since you seem to have all the answers," I snap.

He clenches his fists at his side. "I don't want to fight with you. I was trying to calm you down and strategize about Mom."

"I'm doing everything I can. I want to be doing more, but no one will let me."

"Gee, I wonder why. You're a pain in the ass and we all walk on eggshells around you."

My rage boils over. I swing my fist at him, but he ducks aside.

His eyes flash with anger, but he holds himself in check. "Zeke. Don't."

I want to hit something. I want to scream and kick and throw things until I feel better.

Jordan takes slow steps away from me. "Take a breath."

I lunge at him again and he spins away, grabbing my arm and attempting to hold me against him. I elbow him in the gut and he releases me with an *oof*.

"What the hell are you knuckleheads doing?"

Genny comes out of nowhere and inserts herself between me and Jordan. Her eyes are wild and fiery. She pushes me back with such force that I stumble, taken aback by her sudden appearance.

I look around her and glare at my brother, who is being tugged away by Mackenzie.

"Come, take a walk with me," she tells Jordan, grabbing his arm with both hands and pulling him in the opposite direction.

"Get in the car, Ezekiel." Genny's voice is hard and clear.

I look down at her with surprise. "I–"

"Get. In. The. Car."

I'm pissed off but decide it's not worth it to press her. I climb into her car and slam the passenger door behind me.

Chapter 40

Genny

I was ready to put Zeke through a wall.

Miles had messaged the group chat about Elaine's interrupted treatment, so I grabbed Mackenzie after school and headed straight to Zeke's. I cut through some side streets to get there faster, and we were only a couple of minutes away when we saw Jordan and Zeke arguing on a sidewalk.

"What the heck are they doing out here?" Mackenzie asks.

"Are they—oh, shit."

I see Zeke take a swing at his brother and quickly pull my car over, throwing it into park.

"You get Jordan," I yell to Mackenzie, sprinting to throw myself between the two of them.

I am furious with him. The emotions of the past month bubble over as we drive to his apartment. I hold myself back from saying anything in the car, because I know I won't be able to stop once I get started.

When we arrive we find Zeke, Miles, and Jordan's cars crowding the driveway.

"I need to go see my mom," Zeke says, opening the car door.

"Absolutely not." I get out and stand in front of him. "You're in no condition to see her after the day she's had."

He attempts to rush by me, and I jump back ahead of him. I am in no mood for his nonsense.

"I'm not a child," he snaps.

"You're acting like one." I cross my arms and stand my ground.

He looks me up and down, and I wonder if he's debating picking me up and physically moving me.

I stare right back.

He scoffs and turns, stomping off towards his apartment.

I breathe out a shaky sigh, tears pricking my eyes, and head into Elaine's house to check on things.

I emerge a half hour later feeling discouraged. Elaine was sleeping, so I spoke with Miles. Her care team is recommending they try one last infusion, at a lower dose, before scrapping that method. I know how much she's hoping to avoid chemo and radiation, so this is a blow.

Jordan and Mackenzie drift in as I'm walking out the door.

"Can we talk?" he asks. His appearance is haggard.

"Yeah, of course." I sit at the kitchen table. "You look like shit."

He barks out a laugh. "I'm sure I do."

"You're still pretty cute," Mackenzie teases.

Jordan winks at her and I swallow a giggle.

I hear a retching sound nearby. I turn to see Miles starting the coffee maker and pretending to vomit.

"Gross, you two. Get out of here with that stuff." He laughs.

Jordan rolls his eyes. "*Anyway*. I'm worried about Zeke."

"Join the club," I mutter.

"I'm *really* worried about him," he continues. "He came completely unhinged when I tried to talk to him about my mom's treatment today. I know how he gets with emotional stuff, but this was way beyond that."

I gnaw on my lip. "I agree. I never would have expected him to hit you like that."

He shrugs. "We roughhouse, all brothers do. But he was angrier than I've ever seen him."

"*Nya:wëh.*" I smile gratefully at Miles when he places a mug of coffee in front of me. "I'm not sure how to get through to him, but I'll try."

"I just hope–" Jordan pauses, his expression pained.

Miles sits between us and shares a look with his brother.

"What?" I ask apprehensively.

Miles sighs. "If my mom's infusions get canceled, we're worried Zeke will fall off the cliff again."

Fear slices through my stomach. "What do you mean?"

Jordan taps against his coffee cup. "This reminds me of how he was right after Dad died. And no one knew how to help him then."

I close my eyes and exhale slowly. Immediately, I feel three sets of hands cover my arms.

"We'll get through this together," Miles insists. "We've learned a lot about how to support Mom, and we can do the same for Zeke."

We wrap up the conversation and I give Mackenzie the keys so she can head home. Jordan's going to stay at the house so Miles can get a break.

I climb the steps to Zeke's apartment with a heaviness in my step.

I come in to find the living area empty. I'm boiling some hot water for tea when Zeke emerges from the bedroom.

"Hey," he says, hands in his pockets.

"Hey." I search the cupboards for some tea options to calm my shattered nerves.

He pulls out a chair and sits at the kitchen table, watching me. He looks bedraggled, as though he never showered after the gym and then went on a bender. Which may very well be the case.

I lean against the counter as the water slowly comes to temperature.

"I'm sorry, Gen," he says regretfully. "For all of this."

His tone makes my stomach drop.

"What do you mean?" I ask, and my voice cracks.

He looks down at his hands. "I dragged you into this mess."

"What mess?"

"This." He gestures around the room. "All the time and effort you've put into keeping my family afloat. All this stress. Me."

I sit down next to him. "You're a mess, but you're *my* mess," I reassure him with a squeeze of his hand. "I would do it all again in a heartbeat."

Zeke isn't looking at me, and my heart rate is increasing.

"It's not OK," he mutters. "I'm putting you through too much."

"You're not," I disagree.

"I am!" He stands up and starts to pace. "I see how tired you are. You deal with ten year olds all day and then have to come here and prop me up."

"And I'm happy to do it," I insist, "because I love you."

His head snaps over to look at me. We've always loved each other, of course, but the official proclamation of those three words had not yet happened.

"I think you should consider seeing a therapist," I suggest as I watch him pace. "You're reliving some hard stuff right now, and a professional could help yo–"

"I'm broken, Gen." His eyes are haunted. "I can't be who you need. Who you deserve."

"Don't say that," I whisper.

"It's true."

The tea kettle is whistling but my body won't move.

Zeke comes over to grab the kettle, shuffling awkwardly away from me afterwards.

"It's *not* true," my voice shakes as I stand up from the table. "I've waited my whole life to be where we are now. I will not give up on you just because things got hard."

"I wish you would," he rasps. "I don't deserve you."

"Don't do this again," I beg, reaching for him. "Please. Don't give up on us."

I wrap my arms around his waist, but he stands motionless. Tears are rapidly gathering in my eyes.

"I think we should take a break." His voice sounds hollow.

My head falls forward onto his chest. I want to stay and fight, to convince him that the only place in the world I want to be is with him. But I've been hanging on for dear life for weeks, trying to persuade him to accept my love and support. I've been fighting him and fighting *for* him for years.

"This time was supposed to be different," I whisper.

Zeke looks at the floor. He blinks rapidly but doesn't respond.

I step back from him, biting the inside of my cheek to keep from crying. "OK, then." I grab my jacket from the back of a chair. "I won't beg you to stay with me."

I flee as quickly as I can before the tears overflow.

Chapter 41

Zeke

What have I done?

I regret letting Genny leave the instant she's gone, but my shame prevents me from going after her. Here I am again, ruining the life of the woman who has loved me more than anyone. The disgust I feel towards myself makes my skin crawl.

I get in my car and start driving. I wind up at Wes' apartment on the verge of hurling. He takes me in and keeps me functioning for days, forcing me to eat, shower, and go to the gym. He drives me to the airport so I can catch my flight to Denver, even though he's back on the practice squad and not playing with the team this weekend. I hate myself even more for leaving my mom and brothers with only a text to let them know I won't be home until next week.

Jamie and Sawyer are waiting for me at the gate when my plane lands, even though I know their flight from Toronto got in over an hour ago.

"Come on, man," Jamie gives me a quick hug. "Let's get you a beer and some sleep."

"Wes told us," Sawyer explains, seeing the confusion on my face.

I was lucky to have such caring friends. I feel completely unworthy of them.

They roll me back into the hotel later that night after multiple beers at the team dinner. Jamie's my roommate on this trip, and he's in full Team Dad mode.

"Take these and drink all this water," he tells me, placing a couple aspirin and two bottles of water on the nightstand.

"I'm not drunk," I insist.

"Doesn't matter. Painkillers and water help with broken hearts, too."

I do as I'm told, chugging the water before sitting back against the headboard. I'm restless and too awake to sleep.

What am I going to do once I'm back in Cattaraugus? Getting through this weekend's game will be tough, but at least I'm out of my home environment and routines. The thought of being back in my apartment with all its memories of Genny makes me want to throw up. I could probably stay with Wes or another friend next week, but then I wouldn't be around to support my mom. All I want to do is hide from reality, but that just increases my guilt and shame.

"Have you considered calling her?" Jamie asks gently, taking his book off the nightstand.

"I can't imagine she would answer."

"You don't know that."

I sigh, closing my eyes in pain. "What the hell would I even say? 'Sorry I had a mental breakdown and made your worst nightmare come true again'?"

"I'd probably lead with 'I love you and I fucked up,' personally."

My chest physically hurts from the loss of her. "I love her so much, Jammer. What the fuck is wrong with me?"

Jamie sets down the Indigenous dark fiction anthology he's reading. "Well, I'd argue there's nothing *wrong* with you. But you had a major trauma in early adulthood that altered how you cope with stress."

"You and Wes are cut from the same cloth, man." I shake my head at him. "You two are natural uncles."

He chuckles. "I've got 10+ years of uncle experience on that kid."

I smile for the first time in days.

"Seriously though," Jamie continues, "you should really consider seeing a therapist. You're stuck in some old patterns, and a professional could help you work through those."

"Like what?"

"You broke up with the love of your life, for starters. And you're talking to me about it instead of begging her to forgive you." He smiles fondly at me. "You put too much pressure on yourself, and of course you fall apart. We're meant to live in community, not as individuals."

I exhale loudly. "I thought I was doing better. I thought this time would be different."

"I've been there. Real change takes time and uncomfortable work."

The problem is, I thought I *had* changed. I had Genny to talk to and support me. My entire family and community pitched in to help with my mom's needs during treatment. I thought I should feel radically different this time around, but the result was the same. Why?

I lay flat and throw a pillow over my eyes, trying to manifest sleep. It went about as successfully as I expected. Twenty minutes later, I toss the pillow away and get out of bed.

Jamie looks over his reading glasses at me. "You good?"

"I'm going to shower." I walk past him to the bathroom. "Need a change of scenery."

The hot stream of water beats down on my back, the tiny pinpricks of heat alerting me to how numb I feel everywhere else. The numbness is what I remember most from the months and years after my dad's death. To feel it creep back into my body has freaked me out more than any part of this newest experience with cancer. Ten years ago I didn't recognize my struggle for what it was. Slowly crawling out of the black hole of depression took its toll on me, and finally being free of it the past year or two has been transformative.

Now it's back, and I feel hopeless. The darkness sits on my chest like a weighted blanket each day, and its twisted tendrils worm their way into my thoughts and emotions. I don't want to be apart from Genny, but trapping her in this miserable existence with me feels unreasonable.

I lay in bed afterwards, feeling slightly drowsier from the shower. The events of the past week run through my mind at rapid speed. The situation with Genny is a colossal mess and too painful to dwell on in the moments before sleep, but I know there are more straightforward circumstances I can do something about.

The next morning I make a couple phone calls before heading to practice: a mea culpa to Jordan, and a voicemail for the health clinic back home.

Chapter 42

Genny

This time, heartbreak feels like dying.

Zeke's dad's death was sudden, but the first end of our friendship was gradual over the course of a year. It was confusing and frustrating, like trying to finish a puzzle before realizing you're missing pieces. This second breakup was swift and even more devastating.

Mackenzie and my mom peeled me off the floor the rest of the week, but I made it to school. Jordan gave us the heads up Zeke had disappeared to a friend's place, so I came by most days to check on Elaine and the boys. Life keeps humming along, but inside I'm broken and bruised.

I gave my phone to Mackenzie so that I'm not constantly tempted to check it for calls and messages. I thought Zeke would contact me immediately, but as the days tick by I confront the possibility of a more permanent split. I miss him so much it makes me sick, but I don't want to beg him to have me in his life. I've done that already, and it just left me feeling inadequate and cast off.

I sometimes wonder if my dating life would have been better if I hadn't felt so insecure about myself after Zeke and I stopped being friends. My taste in men took a nosedive once he was no longer in my life, dooming my romantic experiences from the start. Logically, I knew that Zeke moving on with his life had little to do with me, but I couldn't help but take it personally.

Reuniting with him as an adult helped me make sense of those hard years. It felt fated, as though we were holding space in our lives until we could grow up and find each other again. Now none of it felt right. *What was even the point of the past three months if he was just going to break me again?*

I'm so upset with myself for falling into this trap. I'd successfully kept him away from my heart for years. I knew getting close to him again was dangerous, but I'd allowed myself to indulge. He had felt safe, but he wasn't. I would be overthinking how to open my heart again for a long time.

I pour myself into everything that keeps my mind off Zeke. The weather is breaking for spring, so I run nearly every day. Chelsea comes to visit the weekend after things broke down with Zeke. She gives me a crash course in beading, helping me design and create some basic earrings. My fingers ache satisfactorily at the end of each evening as I churn out pair after pair for myself and loved ones.

Keeping myself afloat has become a full-time job, but I'm putting one foot in front of the other.

Me: *picture of purple and white beaded earrings with abalone shell*

Chels: Those are GORGEOUS! You're learning so fast!

Kenzie: Now I have TWO best friends to harass to make me earrings!

Me: Thanks! I'm pretty proud of them. Still need to edge them, I'm nervous

Chels: You'll do great. I'll come back in a few weeks and bump you up to the next skill level

Me: Thank you, friend. I appreciate all your love and support lately

Chels: <3 <3

Kenzie: It's good to see you doing something for yourself for once

Me: I think this is more of a disassociation tactic than anything

Kenzie: Maybe. But it's still good medicine. Keep it up

Chapter 43

Zeke

Jordan welcomes me back home the following Sunday with open arms. We had a really good talk while I was in Denver, and I was relieved to hear he wasn't carrying a grudge about our fight. In fact, he seemed more concerned about me than anything else. In my never-ending quest to be everything to everyone, I somehow missed him growing into a family leader and a hell of a man.

"It's good to have you back, Z." He claps me on the back after a hug.

"I thought you might've changed the locks while I was gone." I smile hesitantly.

He chuckles. "I was tempted to, but Mom said no."

I offer him an iced tea from my fridge, and we sit at the kitchen table together. "How's she doing?"

He twists off the cap and tosses it into the trash nearby. "She's worried about tomorrow, but trying to stay positive." He fiddles with the label on the bottle. "I'm really fucking nervous."

"Me too," I admit, a pit brewing in my stomach.

We sit quietly together for a few minutes. I can hear birds chirping loudly outside, a welcome return after the calm of winter.

"Genny's taking Mom to her appointment," Jordan says, taking a slow sip of tea.

I blow out a long exhale. "OK."

"If you'd rather not be around for that, I understand," he says. "I wasn't sure if you were sticking around this week or not."

I fold my hands nervously. "I'm not sure yet. A buddy invited me to stay with him over at Six Nations for a few days, but I also want to be here for Mom."

"You should take some time away if you can get it," he assures me. "I think it's good for you. We can hold down the fort, no problem."

"I feel so guilty for not being here," I reply in a strained voice.

"I know you do. Believe me, I do." He tosses me a lopsided grin and I smile. He sets his bottle down with a clatter. "But you don't need to. We've got a big family, and lots of helpers. Your health is important, too."

I nod, not sure when I'll ever believe that statement.

"Did you know Genny coordinated the entire effort to get Mom help?" Jordan says.

My smile falls.

"She had spreadsheets, a meal train, and a treatment schedule sent out to half our relations within a few hours of hearing Mom's diagnosis," he continues. "She stepped in and pushed us to get organized when we were flailing. We never asked. She just knew what needed to be done."

I rub my forehead. "I don't need to feel any worse about this than I already do, man."

He watches me. "I'm not trying to make you feel bad. Well, maybe a little," he needles.

"I deserve it," I groan, resting my head against the heel of my hand.

"Maybe so," Jordan continues, "but you also deserve happiness. And she makes you happy."

I sigh. "I know. I knew it and I pushed her away, anyway."

"We've kept a lot from you about Genny over the years," he says. "I think that may have been a mistake. We were trying to protect you, but then you didn't have all the information and made decisions based on what little you knew."

"I don't know that it would've made a difference," I admit. "I was depressed and didn't realize it for years. I wasn't capable of doing anything other than surviving back then."

He puts a hand on my shoulder. "I'm sorry, Zeke. We really failed you."

I look up at him and shake my head. "You didn't. We all suffered and were doing our best. Things are so much better now." I squeeze his hand and he smiles sadly.

After family dinner that night, I start packing to head across the Canadian border and spend a few days with Jamie and Sawyer. I'm not entirely comfortable leaving my family, but I completely trust Genny and my brothers in my absence. This feels like a helpful exercise for me in surrender.

One day at a time, I remind myself.

Chapter 44

Genny

"Let's make some strawberries."

Chelsea has come back for another visit. She and Mackenzie have been keeping me sane the past few weeks, and I treasure their friendship while I'm fighting to get through each day.

Mackenzie is off visiting some college friends this weekend, so Chelsea and I are hunkering down for another beadwork crash course.

"Yes!" I clap eagerly. "I'm excited to learn how to make more complicated designs."

Chelsea starts setting up the supplies she brought with her on the kitchen table while I rummage in the kitchen for snacks and drinks. I bring out a bowl of popcorn, some cornbread, and a bottle of wine.

"You're always so fancy with your wine," Chelsea teases, happily accepting a glass. "I only ever have beer just laying around."

I chuckle and arrange the food. "I like beer, too. I just haven't been in the mood for it lately."

We snack and bead while savoring the fresh air coming in through the windows. The weather has been warming up, and daffodils are pushing through the dirt. It feels like spring everywhere but in my heart, which is stuck firmly in winter.

"How are you feeling today?" Chelsea asks, glancing up at me while she tacks down a line of beads.

I sigh. "About the same, I guess. Terrible. Horrible. But I'm also sick of feeling that way, and want to be myself again."

She nods, threading her needle with more beads. "I've never loved anyone the way you love Zeke, so it feels easy to say that things will keep getting better with time." She pushes her needle through the backing fabric. "But I have to believe that's still true."

I set my needle down briefly and take a sip from my wine glass. "I'm sure it is. And I've done this before. I've already gotten over him once."

Chelsea winces, and I'm not certain if it's from my words or pricking her finger. "There's more to get over now though, I suppose."

No kidding. I try to push Zeke from my mind during the day, but falling asleep at night is a mental minefield. Memories of our relationship flood my brain as I lay with my eyes closed, and the dreams of him are even worse. I miss his smile, his touch, his strong arms. I miss looking forward to our time together on weekends and how much he makes me laugh with our easy banter. I can't wait until I no longer mourn those echoes of us.

"How are *you* feeling?" I ask, knowing it has only been a few months since her own breakup.

She scoffs. "I'm fine. Glad I don't have to deal with Brock anymore." She sets down her beadwork and reaches for the popcorn. "Honestly, I cannot deal with another lacrosse player."

"They're not all bad," I protest, but cringe after grabbing a handful of popcorn from the bowl she offered. "Well, maybe I need to revise my thinking on that."

Chelsea laughs. "See? Nothing but trouble!"

I pop some kernels in my mouth. "Wes is nice," I say pointedly.

She rolls her eyes. "Wes *seems* nice. That's how they getcha."

"Well, I've seen no red flags from him so far." I brush my hands off over a napkin. "The man is a walking *green* flag."

She snorts. "I've thought that before." She picks her beadwork back up. "How's your strawberry coming along?"

I head out for a walk the next day after Chelsea leaves. I'm craving some fresh air and alone time to work through my thoughts.

I'm grateful to have a new hobby to keep me occupied, and it makes me realize that I haven't really *had* hobbies in...a while? Ever? I always make time for fitness, but otherwise I fill my days with busyness outside of work. I spend so much time on others, which I love doing, but I've let that creep into all of my free hours. I'm out of balance. Even while I was with Zeke, *he* became my hobby, often at the expense of taking care of myself.

My miles and gym time had flatlined when I was spending every evening with him after Elaine's diagnosis. I'm increasingly feeling like somewhere along the way I've lost myself. Being single again may be an opportunity to reconnect, even while I'm still grieving the loss of Zeke.

I return to the house and smile at the sight of our car in the driveway. Mackenzie's home. I was looking forward to catching up on our weekend activities. Tomorrow is Monday, a new week, and a new chance for a fresh start.

Chapter 45

O'nót'ah

April

Zeke

Spring is here, and Creation is waking up.

It's been three weeks since Genny and I split. There's a hole in my life where she used to be, but I'm doing my best to make each day a little better than the day before.

I started seeing a therapist and, much to my dismay, I could see that it was going to really help. There was a lot of work to do, but I could tell that the experience would bear fruit. Jamie was right—I couldn't deal with my mom's illness by simply hoping I would handle it better.

Genny had taken my mom to her next infusion, and the treatment had finally gone well. She was regaining some of her appetite and energy. We were cautiously optimistic that she'd be

249

able to tolerate the remaining infusions, which raised my spirits and calmed my nerves.

The Outlaws had squeaked into the playoffs with a handful of key wins at the end of the season, and it helped me to have high stakes games to focus on. Wes was back on the starting roster, and it looked like he was there for good. He was scoring goals and making big defensive plays, proving himself invaluable for the postseason.

Things are turning around in my life in many ways, and I'm deeply thankful. But fuck, I miss Genny so damn much.

It's Sunday and Wes is coming over for family dinner. We'd adopted him as part of the family since training camp, and I was glad to provide him with the community I know he misses back home in Wisconsin.

My mom looks weak and tired, but she's happy. Ezra drove down from Geneseo for the weekend, so the wolf pack is fully represented.

"And our bear friend, too," she embraces Wes, noting his mother's clan in the Oneida Nation. "We've got a full den tonight."

We dig into dinner, still blessed to have a fridge full of meals from friends who replenished us each week. My brothers have a lot of questions about our upcoming playoff opponent, the Georgia Hive.

We're nearing the end of our meal when an uncomfortable silence falls across the table. I glance up to find every single person looking at me.

"What's going on?" I ask nervously. "Mom, are you OK?"

She clears her throat. "I'm fine. We just...wanted to talk to you."

Panic rises in my throat like bile, and I send all my focus into taking deep breaths to calm down. "Is everything all right?"

"Everything's OK, but we know that you're not," Ezra says.

Hearing that from my youngest brother gets my attention. I open my mouth to disagree, but the words aren't there.

"Why did you break up with Genny, you absolute dumbass?" Jordan asks, his voice kind despite his phrasing.

I grimace. "I know I screwed up."

"Yeah, you did," Miles agrees. "Now, what are you going to do to fix it?"

I shake my head, looking down at my empty plate. "I don't know if I can." My eyes blink back tears. "I don't deserve her. She trusted me after I did this in the past, and then I went and did it again."

My mom scoots her chair beside me. "Genny's really hurt right now. She needs time, but I think she'd be willing to hear you out eventually." She squeezes my hand. "She loves you just as much as I do, Zeke."

"She's part of our family," Miles points out. "She's done so much for us over the years that you don't know about, because we didn't want to upset you."

I frown. "I know about the stuff with Mom's cancer support. What else is there?"

"She was my math tutor during middle school and high school," Ezra says. "I was really struggling, and she'd come over every week to encourage me and explain concepts in a way I could understand."

"I couldn't have played baseball in high school if she hadn't offered to drive me to games and practices," Miles pipes in. "Mom had to work and drive Jordan around for lacrosse, so Genny would leave class early to take me."

"She taught me how to drive," Jordan says.

"She's spent so much time with me and your mother," my grandmother chimes in. "I've especially treasured her companionship since your grandfather died. She's such a bright spot in my weeks."

"She would come over to help with all kinds of things when she knew you wouldn't be here," Jordan adds. "She realized you didn't want to maintain your friendship, but she never stopped loving us and giving us her time."

"She's like a sister to us," Miles says emphatically, "and we don't want this to drive her away."

My heart is already in tatters, but hearing more about Genny's devotion to my family ripped those shreds into tinier pieces. I'm stuck in an endless loop of missing her and beating myself up for ending things. I lay my torso down on the table, my head on my forearms. I had the best woman in the world, and I'd tossed her away. Twice.

"You're worthy of her love, Zeke," my grandmother says, reaching across the table to place her hand on my arm. "No matter how you feel right now, you're a good man and we know that. We all appreciate everything you do for us."

"We don't tell you that enough," Ezra interjects. "You helped Mom raise us, at least me and Miles, and you're such an inspiration to me."

Tears sting my eyes, and I lean over to grab his hand. "Same to you, kid. You're doing way better in school than I ever did."

My family piles on me for hugs and I feel a lifting in my soul. We're all learning how to best love each other, not just me.

Their intervention comes to a close as we begin cleaning up after dinner. I'm not sure that I feel much better, but I know I can't avoid Genny any longer.

I've resisted reaching out to her, even though I regret sending her away with every fiber of my being. I feel such deep shame about how I acted that day and in the month leading up to it. My depression is no longer raging completely unchecked, but deeply examining my thoughts and actions is still very new for me. Facing Genny has felt impossible, so I've run from it. But it's yet another way that I've been unfair to her, and I need to take accountability for my shittiness.

It's getting late, but I'm crawling out of my skin to talk to her. After dinner I head to her house and knock on the front door, drawing in a ragged breath.

Mackenzie opens. Her eyes widen in surprise before she slams the door shut.

"Kenz," I plead, knocking again. "Please."

I hear her footsteps moving around quickly, and a couple of voices.

The door cracks back open. "What do you want, Zeke?" she asks.

"Is Genny home?"

"That depends on what you want."

I sigh. "I want to tell her I'm an idiot and beg her to consider forgiving me."

Mackenzie narrows one eye at me. "None of this sounds like new information."

"Please, Kenzie," I whisper hoarsely. "I need her to know this isn't her fault. She did nothing wrong, and I am so remorseful over asking her to leave. I don't deserve her forgiveness, but I can't go another day without trying."

Her eyes soften. "I'll tell her. But I don't think she wants to talk to you right now."

I nod. "I understand. Thank you for asking."

The door closes again and I wait on the stoop. My mind replays our first kiss here, right after the first time I'd begged her to forgive me and try again. *I am the world's biggest jerk.* The urge to give up and go home is strong, but I fight it.

The doorknob turns and I eagerly look up, hope springing in my heart.

Mackenzie looks back at me once more. She shakes her head sadly. "I'm sorry, Zeke. She doesn't want to see you."

My insides crumble. The reality of Genny's loss is hitting even harder now that she's so close.

"Can't say that I blame her," I smile weakly. "Thanks for trying."

Mackenzie pokes her head out further. "Fight for her, Zeke," she says quietly. "She needs to know if you're willing to fight through the hard stuff."

A pinprick of light emerges in my core. "I will."

"But if you hurt her again I'm not opening the door next time."

Chapter 46

Genny

I scan the parking lot for Zeke's car as I pull in. *Phew.* No sign of him.

I'm tired of coming to the gym at odd hours, but I'm also not ready to face him. So, here I am at 10pm with just enough time to get in a workout before the building closes.

It's late April, a month and a half since Zeke and I split. The pain is still there, but throwing myself back into my routines has helped keep it at bay for longer stretches. He came by the house a few weeks ago, but I didn't want to see him. I was still emotionally fragile and didn't want to be upset by him or, even worse, agree to give things another shot. *Been there, done that.*

The next morning, I found two cups of coffee waiting for me on the porch after my run. We didn't know who it was from, but of course had our suspicions. The next day was a repeat, this time with a note from Zeke. He'd left coffee on our doorstep most mornings since then, notes tucked underneath the cup reserved for me. I'd wanted to throw away both the coffee and the notes, but Mackenzie convinced me to store the papers until I was ready to read them. And to never waste a hot cup of Tim's.

I'm so angry with myself for letting him back into my life. My boundaries went to shit after Elaine's diagnosis. I should have protected myself, but I convinced myself I could save him this time. Of course I couldn't. Zeke didn't want to be saved.

I shake my head to come back to the present. I dump my bag in a gym cubby and pop my headphones on. I desperately need some loud, angsty music and heavy weights.

I'm pulling up my playlist when I catch sight of Wes near the dumbbells. He smiles sheepishly at me and I freeze, my eyes darting around to see if Zeke is with him. I don't see him, but now I'm on edge.

I claim one of the open racks and start setting up my barbell, exhaling shakily. How am I going to exist in my town if I'm constantly looking over my shoulder? Once the bar is ready, I sit on the weight bench and catch my breath.

I'm getting my notes app ready to keep track of my weights and reps when Wes squats down in front of me, his headphones around his neck. I jump in surprise.

"Sorry," he apologizes, "I tried not to scare you, especially at this time of night."

"It's ok," I exhale, setting my phone and headphones down on the bench next to me. "What's up?"

"You looked nervous when you saw me, so I wanted to check in on you," he explains kindly.

I sigh. "It's not you. It's –"

"Zeke. Yeah, I figured."

I look down at my hands, fidgeting with my thumbs.

"He's not with me," Wes assures. "He's not a night owl like I am."

I smile, feeling relieved.

"How are you doing, Genny?" he asks, his voice softening.

Tears prick at the corners of my eyes as I look up and around. "Not great," I whisper in response. "Not horrible, either. But it's a lot."

He raises himself to sit next to me on the bench and slides my things over. "Want a hug?"

I nod and he immediately wraps me in a bear hug. I squeeze him back, my tears spilling onto his damp t-shirt. He holds me and pats my back, not rushing me through the outpouring of emotion.

"I'm sorry," I sniff, wiping my tears and nose with the back of my hand.

"You've got nothing to be sorry for," Wes says. "I hate seeing you in so much pain."

I laugh ironically. "It's not my first time being down bad, crying at the gym."

He watches me as I pull myself back together. "You're not the only one. He's been a mess."

I continue wiping my eyes, unsure of how to respond.

"I can't figure this out for him," I eventually say. "He knows I love him and want to be there for him, but I can't make him want me."

Wes nods slowly. "You're right. You two have already been through this."

"Yeah." I swallow, heartbreak settling deep into my chest.

He stretches his legs in front of him. "He started seeing a therapist. Not sure if you knew that."

My mouth pops open in shock. "Seriously? Zeke?"

Wes smiles. "I was surprised, too. But, yeah. He's been opening up to me a lot more lately, which is good to see."

"Wow." I'm truly stunned. "Well, I'm really glad to hear that."

"Me too. He's doing some important healing." He slaps his hands on his thighs and stands up. "Well, I'll let you get back to your workout." He nudges my foot with his green Converse sneaker. "Promise me you'll reach out if you need anything, OK?"

"I promise." I stand and give him one last hug. "Thanks for being such a good friend, Wes."

"Anytime," he smiles, pulling his headphones on and heading back to the dumbbells.

Zeke is in therapy? I'm not sure anything would have shocked me more than hearing that. He'd talked to me about his past and his emotions more than he ever had while we were together, but that had completely vanished once his mom got sick. He's reserved with most people, even those he's close with. I desperately wish he would have sought grief counseling while he was in college, instead of leaning further into his downward spiral. Is it possible he's learning from his mistakes?

I can't dwell on it. Of course I'm happy to hear he's taking steps to work on his mental health, but ultimately it doesn't involve me. I hope he makes progress on his healing journey, but it means nothing until or unless he changes his life. And I can't wait around hoping for that to happen. It's time for me to really and truly move on.

I wave at Wes as he leaves the gym, not sure if or when I'll see him again. There's a heaviness in my chest, but also a determination to go forward on a fresh path.

Chapter 47

Ganŏ'gat

May

Zeke

The Outlaws are heading to the Championship.

It's an unbelievable turn of events after barely making the playoffs, but we got hot at the right time. Our power play has been unstoppable, and everyone is contributing to goal scoring. Sawyer, Jamie, and I have been firing on all cylinders, playing on a line together that's leading the team in points. My game feels like it's clicked into the next level, as I'm playing looser and more confident than I ever have.

The team is leaving today for Calgary, our championship opponent. Coach wants to give us a day to adjust to the time change before practice on Thursday, and then the game on Friday. After that it's right back to Buffalo, where we'll play

Game 2 on Sunday in front of a home crowd. It's a best-of-3 series, and we're taking it one game at a time.

In-between playing and training, I've been dedicating my time to my mom's care and working through what I'm processing in therapy each week. I've found myself writing more than I ever have. I'm filling pages of a notebook each day, detailing memories and situations that I'm struggling with. Many times, this involves my relationship with Genny. I started separating those out and writing them as letters to her directly, wanting to share where my head has been and how I'm working on retraining my thoughts. I tucked these in with the cups of coffee I was leaving on her porch each morning, hoping she would be willing to read them. I haven't heard from her, so I'm not sure if she has or will. But I keep writing.

I haven't had a chance to leave her coffee yet this week with all of our championship preparations. Given my travel, it would have to wait until I was back in town. I prayed she wouldn't think I'd given up on her.

I want Genny back more than I want my next breath. I also want to respect her wishes for time and space. My daily coffee deliveries have switched from hot to iced on account of the weather, but otherwise I haven't reached out. Texting or calling felt like intrusions. It's probably time to stop by again, and this time I'll ask Mackenzie if I should quit it with the beverages. I won't give up waiting for her, but I don't want to cause her pain by leaving such visual reminders each day, either.

I doodle in a notebook on the flight out west. I always had a knack for drawing, but never pursued it since sports took up so much of my time. I scribble a lacrosse stick with my pencil, and my brain relaxes.

"We should really dial into our spiritual connection to lacrosse as we approach the Championship," Jamie had encouraged me and Wes after our last practice. "It's more than a game to the Haudenosaunee. It's in our blood and in our hearts, because the Creator gave it to us."

Wes nodded. "I thought about that a lot while I was up and down on the practice roster. I've had to train both my body and my mind to stay focused. Letting go of what I can't control has been good medicine."

"That's a good perspective," I said. "I never thought of it that way." Lacrosse had become a means to an end in providing for my family, and I'd lost touch with its traditional principles.

Jamie tapped Wes with his stick. "It teaches us discipline. We learn a lot about ourselves by playing." He clapped me on the shoulder as he walked past my locker stall. "And we play for those who no longer can, as well."

"Hey, that looks great!" Wes says from his seat next to me on the plane. He'd been reading on his Kindle but places it on the seat back tray. "I didn't know you liked to draw."

I smile, shading out a player holding the stick I'd made. "I do, but I haven't done it in years. I'm always too busy."

He watches me sketch with interest. "You're never too busy to do something that gives you joy and energy. I bring a book everywhere with me so I can sneak in some reading whenever I have a few minutes. It helps keep me calm."

I nod. "You're right. I should probably make some time for stuff like this."

"You're talented," Wes says, picking his Kindle back up. "You should take a class or something."

"That would be fun." I make a mental note to check out the Community Center offerings for art once I'm back in town.

We touch down in Calgary and reunite with the rest of the team. The grand adventure has begun.

Chapter 48

Genny

I hated the daily coffees from Zeke until they stopped coming.

I jogged back to the house on Monday morning expecting to see the two familiar red cups in front of the door. I don't know how he did it, but he always impeccably timed his deliveries during my run. On that day, however, the porch was empty.

I thought I would feel relieved, but instead I was disappointed. I may not have felt ready to talk to Zeke yet, but I enjoyed knowing he thought about me every day. It was a mini validation that he knew he was wrong.

The following morning was the same. I came back from my run--no coffee. I officially felt depressed about it once Wednesday rolled around.

"Maybe he's dead," Mackenzie says, chugging a travel mug of homemade coffee before we exit the car for work.

"Don't joke," I chastise her.

Maybe he's given up on me, I wonder throughout the day. I plaster a smile on my face for my students, but it doesn't reach my eyes. The thought that he's moved on brings me to my knees, stirring up panic and regret in my stomach.

Don't be ridiculous, I curse myself. *This is what you wanted. You don't want to get pulled back into his orbit.* It felt selfish to feel upset about this. If Zeke is moving on, then that's a good thing. He lives his life stuck in the past, and going forward without me could be the best thing for him. That thought brings me little comfort.

By the time the school day is over I feel sick from winding myself up.

"Maybe you should read his letters," Mackenzie suggests gently as I spiral in the car. I'm busy inventing plausible scenarios to explain why he hasn't reached out in days.

"What could he possibly have to say that I haven't already heard or considered?" I ask morosely.

She parks and turns towards me. "I think a lot depends on what he's done with himself and his life since he ended things. If nothing has changed, then nothing *will* change if you two got back together."

"I can't keep repeating this same cycle with him."

"Definitely not." Her eyes are sympathetic. "Do you miss him?"

"So damn much, Kenzie." I bite my lip, rapidly blinking back tears.

"You seem freaked out that he stopped bringing you apology coffees."

"I am. I didn't expect to be." I sigh shakily.

"I think that means you're ready to hear what he has to say."

"I don't know." I look down at my hands. "I'm afraid if I read his words I'll lose all the work I've done to heal the past two months."

"That's not the Genny I know. You've had anti-Zeke guards posted around the walls of your heart for over a decade."

"But then I let him in," I whisper.

"Because you *love* him. And he loves you." Mackenzie squeezes my hand. "You gave things another shot even though you were scared. And I'm so proud of you for that, no matter how things ended."

I swallow. "I would have regretted not trying again."

"Will you regret not hearing him out this time?"

Once we're inside, she brings me the stack of Zeke's notes she's been keeping in her room at my request. Seeing them all in one place makes me realize how many there are. *Gulp.*

"Let me know if you need me, OK?" Mackenzie gives me a quick hug before leaving me to it.

My fingers tremble as they hold the top letter, turning it over in my hands. Reading these means I have to do something about my feelings, rather than continue avoiding them at all costs. I take a deep breath and unfold the paper.

Genny,

I don't know if you'll read this. I hope you do.

I'm not much of a writer. You know that. But I wanted to share what I was thinking about today after I left my therapist's office. I've been going once or twice a week, and I should've started back when you first suggested it years ago. We talked about times in my life that I felt safe, and made a plan for how I could tap into those memories when life feels out of my control.

Almost every memory I thought of involved you. Walking you home after playing all day as kids. The way you listened while I was trying to decide between attending Hopkins or Syracuse. Your smile and kiss on the cheek when you accepted my invitation to the prom.

I've lost a lot of memories from the first few months after my dad died. My therapist says that's common with traumatic experiences. But I remember, clear as day, when you sat with me on the bench by the athletic fields and told me it was OK to not be OK. That you'd make sure my family was taken care of after I left. You held my hand and just sat with me, even though I was angry and silent. I remember how my body relaxed knowing that you were there.

You made me feel safe at the beginning of my mom's cancer battle. Your presence and your touch were the only things that calmed me down and allowed me to live in the present instead of being fearful of the future. I was still scared underneath it all, though, and it brought back a lot of old pain. I was so afraid to lose you that I chased you away before you could hurt me. Being in danger of losing a second parent felt like I could lose anybody that was close to me, and no one was closer than you. If I didn't lose you to illness or an accident, I knew I'd lose you to my demons. I knew I was doing it, but I couldn't stop myself.

I'm so sorry, Gen. A piece of me is missing without you. You're my best friend and I know there's no one else for me. I'm going to keep writing to you so I can tell you how much I regret hurting you again and again. I understand it may never be enough.

I love you.
Zeke

The lined paper slips from my fingers and onto the bed. I open the next note, and the next. They're all a version of this, a cross between diary entry and love letter. I expected regret, but they're also filled with joy, peace, and understanding. I can see him connecting the dots between painful experiences in his life, and recognizing how his reactions led to situations becoming even worse. Wes was right; he was doing the work to better himself.

My tears splatter over the papers as I finish reading. I'm so incredibly proud of him.

My heart is racing, feeling three sizes larger than usual. I grab my keys and head out, not waiting for my mind to change.

Zeke's car isn't in the driveway when I arrive at his place. *Dammit.* Our timing has always sucked. I hear my name and look across the passenger seat to see Elaine waving at me from her back garden. She looks fatigued but cheerful among the yellow buttercups.

"You look like you're feeling well today," I smile, getting out of the car.

"For now I am, yes." She embraces me extra tightly. "Are you looking for Zeke?"

I smile sheepishly. "Is he out?"

"He left for Calgary early this morning."

I furrow my brow. "Calgary? On a Wednesday?"

"It's Championship weekend," Elaine explains.

"Oh. Oh!" In my heartbreak, I'd stopped watching Outlaws games or following their progress. I'd realized they made the playoffs when the school held a spirit day for kids and staff to wear Outlaws gear, but I had otherwise put it out of mind.

Zeke had dreamed of playing for an NLL championship since we were kids. We used to score goals in the backyard, pretending we were the legendary Gait brothers winning it all for Philadelphia and Detroit. My body hums with joy that he's getting to experience this for real.

"I don't expect he'll be home until after Sunday night's game," she continued. "He's staying with the team in Buffalo between Games 1 and 2."

My stomach sank. I could already feel my determination crumbling.

"You could call him," she suggested gently. "I know he'd be happy to hear from you."

I shake my head. "It's OK. I don't want to bother him while he's getting ready for such an important game."

"I'd invite you to Sunday's game with us, but I'm out of tickets." She smiles at me regretfully.

"Don't worry about it," I assure her quickly. "I'm not sure if I'll be watching or not."

Her eyes are sad as she looks at me. "I understand."

I shuffle my feet. "Can I do anything for you before I go?"

"I'm all set. Jordy's here in case I need anything."

I head back home, my thoughts swirling. Mackenzie accosts me the instant I'm past the front door.

"Did you go see Zeke?" she asks eagerly.

I shake my head. "He wasn't home, and he's out of town until late Sunday night." I flop onto the couch with a sigh.

"Geez, they already left for Calgary?"

I narrow my eyes at her.

"Listen, I'm not the one nursing a broken heart over an Outlaws player. I've been following all their games on social media when you weren't looking."

I laugh, feeling a twinge of lightness for the first time in weeks.

"The letters were significant, I take it?" Mackenzie sinks into the couch next to me.

I nod.

"So, what are you going to do?"

I close my eyes in frustration. "I don't know."

"What were you going to say to him, if you'd seen him tonight?"

I look across the room, my eyes unfocused. "That I was proud of him for asking for help. And that I would always love him, no matter what happens between us."

We're silent for a minute, both of us deep in thought.

"I think you need to call him," Mackenzie says quietly. "If you don't want to, then you should go to the game on Sunday."

I shake my head. "I can't talk to him right now and risk distracting him in the middle of the championship games."

"Then I guess we're going to Buffalo on Sunday."

My heart skips a beat at the thought. "How? Elaine's using all her family seats, and I can't imagine there are any tickets left to buy."

"Let me deal with that," she says. "I know a guy."

"What kind of rezzy ticket scalper do you know?" I groan.

"Let me see what I can do."

Chapter 49

Zeke

The Outlaws won Game 1 in Calgary by the skin of our teeth.

We hung around with the Stampede all game, keeping it close with goals being scored back and forth. That thrilled us going into the fourth quarter, since Calgary was one of the league's best teams this year. The Outlaws were here as Cinderellas going on a magical run against all odds.

With five minutes left, Sawyer went sailing in front of the net, sending the ball past the goaltender before his body hit the crease. We defended that one goal lead for the rest of the game. Multiple players blocked shots with their bodies and took hard contact from the Stampede to keep the ball out of our net.

Calgary was pissed. Their early play in the game suggested they didn't take us seriously and expected to have an easy path to the championship. We exploited their sloppiness and soft defense at every opportunity, pulling out the big win. We knew we'd pay for it in Game 2 back home, but that was a problem for another day.

Everyone is sore and exhausted by the time we get to the hotel in Buffalo on Saturday, ready for dinner and bed. Some guys paid a pretty penny to book appointments for sports massages or cryotherapy for recovery. Wes, Jamie, and I went old school, heading to the hotel gym to roll out our muscles and do some deep stretching before an early bedtime.

My phone rings as I'm working on my hamstrings. Seeing my mom's name on the screen, I quickly answer it.

"Hey, Mom," I say, sitting down against the wall with the foam roller under my leg.

"Hi, Zeke. Everything's OK," she assures me, knowing I worry with every phone call currently. "I just wanted to check on you since you're in-between games."

I breathe a sigh of relief. "I'm good. Getting stretched out before bed."

We chat about last night's game and how everyone is feeling going into Game 2. The city of Buffalo is buzzing in anticipation of tomorrow night.

"Oh, one last thing before I let you go," she says, taking a brief pause before continuing. "Genny stopped by looking for you on Wednesday."

I drop my phone, catching it before it hits the floor where I'm sitting. "Genny?"

Wes looks over, eyebrows raised as he rolls out his quads next to me.

"I wasn't sure if I should tell you," my mom says nervously.

"No, no, I'm glad you did," I reply, my heart racing. "What did she say?"

"She didn't give a reason. I let her know you'd be out of town until after tomorrow's game."

I nod silently, trying to keep a surge of hope at bay.

"What's up?" Jamie asks pointedly after I hang up.

I clear my throat, reaching for my foam roller so I can get back to work. "Nothing much." I start rolling out my IT band along the side of my right thigh. "Genny came by looking for me this week." I give up on trying to hide my smile of delight.

"Yeah!" Wes exclaims, leaning over to give me a high five.

"That seems promising," Jamie says, smiling widely. "It's not too late to call or text tonight, you know."

"I will on Monday," I say. "I need to stay locked in until after Game 2."

Easier said than done.

Chapter 50

Genny

Mackenzie pulled some levers and somehow we acquired three tickets to Game 2 without overpaying too badly. Our mom wanted to come with us, and the three of us spent the past few days sewing matching ribbon skirts in Outlaws colors: orange, white, black, and purple.

I feel sick with anxiety the closer we get to game time. I don't have to talk to Zeke afterwards, but I think I want to. I don't have to suggest getting back together, but I also think I might want to do that.

What if he's moved on? I can't shake the intrusive thought that he's not interested in me anymore. He's clearly going through a period of deep healing and change; what if that extends to his feelings about us?

"You ready to go, Gen?" Mackenzie calls from across the house.

Discarded outfit pieces cover my bed, and I'm struggling to make decisions. I scramble to throw my feet into moccasins and shove a pair of earrings I just made into my purse before rushing out.

The arena is a madhouse when we arrive. Everywhere you look, fans are decked out in Outlaws gear. I'd decided not to wear my jersey because it didn't pair well with my ribbon skirt, but now I'm regretting not having it.

"Do you mind if I pop into the team store real quick?" I ask Mackenzie and my mom. The store is overflowing with people, and I'd rather do just about anything other than brave that crush of humanity.

They wave me on and I launch myself into the store, ducking between aisles and squeezing past people comparing items. I find myself crammed against a rack of jersey t-shirts just like the one I wore at Zeke's our first night together. My heart thumps painfully in my chest at the memory of how much he'd loved seeing me wearing his number.

I flip through the various sizes and options before finding Zeke's number 36 in my size. I throw myself through traffic to reach the checkout and emerge victorious, albeit sweaty from the exertion.

"Got what I needed," I announce, out of breath, my cheeks feeling flushed.

"This is not cute," Mackenzie swirls her finger around in the air in front of me. "Let's find a bathroom and I can do something with your hair."

I change into my new Outlaws shirt and give my sister free rein to tame my loose tresses. She braids two sections before pulling the rest of it up into a twist, pinning the braids around it.

"Were they out of the shirts that specifically say 'Zeke's Girl' on them?" she teases me with bobby pins between her teeth.

I blush. "Stop it!"

She chuckles. "I'm into this Indigenous lacrosse WAG aesthetic, honestly. Do you have earrings?"

I rummage through my purse and pull on the pair I'd made last week. I give her a little twirl with the full look.

"Deadly. Come on, let's go find our seats."

We're on the opposite side of the arena from Zeke's family's seats, and further away from the floor. The view is still pretty decent, all things considered. My mom and Mackenzie leave on a mission to find drinks and snacks while I look around.

The place is hopping. The Outlaws won Game 1, so they can win the championship trophy on home turf tonight. It's been ages since we had a championship team in Buffalo, and the fanbase is hungry. The arena music is pumping, and the atmosphere is charged.

It's the biggest game of Zeke's life. The gravity of the moment hits me and I close my eyes to drink in the humming of happy fans. The city is celebrating and anticipating a big game with a positive outcome.

Regardless of what happens tonight, I'm grateful and glad to be here to celebrate Zeke.

Chapter 51

Zeke

The Hideout is electric. The fans are on their feet and loud as hell during pregame introductions. My eyes scan the crowd until I spot my mom and brothers sitting in their usual seats. I smile and they cheer loudly, waving signs with my name and number on them.

It's a big day for our family after two decades of hard work and struggle. My parents put a lot of time and energy into allowing me to pursue lacrosse as a passion. Money was always tight, and they stretched what they could to make it work. We used what we had and borrowed what we didn't for equipment, but sometimes I just needed new gear. My years in college were challenging so close on the heels of my dad's death, and it was a relief when I graduated with decent grades. I knew that all the hardships I'd been through had brought me here today. I have a successful career as a professional lacrosse player, and I'm knocking on the door of a championship. We may have lost my dad too young, but my mom's still here and fighting. My brothers are happy, healthy, and close with each other. I'm tremendously blessed.

Still, I find myself looking into the crowd for Genny. Hearing that she'd stopped by last week gave me hope that maybe she'd come to tonight's game. It seemed highly unlikely, but there was a chance, right?

She could have been stopping by to tell me to leave her alone, I admit ruefully. Although at the time I hadn't left any letters for her in almost a week, so why would she pick that time to tell me off? Or maybe, as I feared, she thought I was moving on without her. I tried to make my feelings crystal clear in my letters, but who knows if she tossed those immediately into the trash each day.

I will never stop waiting for her. I can't imagine ever finding another woman I could love as much as Genny. My heart belongs to her. We were made for each other.

I continue looking for her during the singing of the national anthems. Nothing. I take a deep breath and turn my focus back to the game.

Beating this Calgary team twice in a row is a tall order, but we're ready for the challenge. We know they're going to come out strong and hungry, and we're prepared for it. I look down the line of players next to me and nod my head at my teammates. The lights come back on full strength and the crowd cheers, anticipating the opening faceoff.

It's going to take 100% effort for the full sixty minutes. If we can do that, I feel confident we'll be lifting that trophy at the end of the night.

Chapter 52

Genny

This game is going to give me a heart attack.

The Calgary Stampede came out like they'd been launched from a cannon: hitting bodies, scooping balls, and making perfect passes all over the floor. The Outlaws are playing a desperate, and very good, team in a dogfight for the ultimate prize.

We fall into an early deficit but pull within three goals at halftime. I'm on edge, still nursing the same beer I started the game with.

"It's going to be tough to play from behind against a team at this level," my mom states, "but I think we're going to see some of that Outlaws magic in the second half." Her eyes sparkle. She's always loved lacrosse, and we've consistently watched the Outlaws as a family since the team's inception in the early 90s.

"And if they don't pull it off, there's Game 3 next weekend in Calgary," Mackenzie points out.

I groan. "I hope not. Those winner-take-all games are so unpredictable."

"Well, we'll see." My mom sits back in her chair to watch the halftime entertainment. Corgis are racing across the arena floor in adorable outfits. "Zeke's playing really well." She sneaks a glance at me.

"He is," I admit with my stomach in knots.

The second half begins and the Outlaws slowly chip away at the Stampede's lead. At one point they're down a player due to penalties, but Wes makes a flying stick check to knock the ball loose and send it trickling over the center line. This triggers an over and back charge, meaning the Stampede loses possession and the shot clock resets to 30 seconds. The Outlaws now have an unexpected offensive possession. They convert and pull within a goal of the Stampede.

The fourth quarter dawns with a chance for the Outlaws on the power play. The team passes the ball quickly and efficiently in the offensive zone. Wes feeds the ball to a streaking Zeke, who out muscles his defender and snipes a shot into the top right corner.

The arena explodes in jubilation at tying the game. The three of us Skye women high five and shout for joy.

Then it's right back to biting my nails, as the Stampede win the faceoff and set up in the Outlaws' zone. They pass with crisp precision but the goalie stonewalls them, making an incredible save before tossing the ball down to the opposite end of the floor.

Jamie battles down low, fighting for the loose ball in the corner. Zeke comes in to help, checking a defender into the boards and kicking the ball loose. Jamie scoops it up, charges at the net, and hits a perfect shot between the goaltender's legs.

If we thought the arena was loud when the Outlaws tied the game, then we were unprepared for the cacophony that erupted when they took the lead. There were five minutes remaining in the fourth quarter, and the championship trophy was so close we could taste it.

Chapter 53

Zeke

The crowd is hyped and we're trying desperately to stay locked in.

All we have to do is play defense for the next five minutes against an incredibly talented team with their backs against the wall. *Piece of cake—not.*

We've got our strategy from the coaches: Keep the ball out of our net, and take as much time off the clock as possible. If we see an exceptional opportunity to score, then take it, but otherwise sit tight and keep the ball out of the Stampede's sticks.

Our defense executes the plan perfectly, laying down their bodies to protect the net and keep the ball tied up in corners. The Stampede are throwing everything they can at us, including an extra attacker when they pull their goalie for an advantage. The shot clock expires and everyone is gasping for breath, eager to make a line change and get fresh legs on the floor. If we play our cards right, we can take the last shot of the game and win as time expires.

I'm high on adrenaline when I come off the bench, running out to cover the far side of the floor. The seconds are ticking down, and I can feel the fans are about to go nuts. Sawyer and Jamie pass the ball back and forth to each other to kill time. A Stampede player makes an aggressive move towards Jamie, while another covers Sawyer, so Jamie passes the ball over to me.

It's a long pass, but a relatively easy one to catch. I raise my stick to grab the ball out of the air, but I misjudge the angle and it hits the top of my stick instead of sinking into the pocket, sending it skittering off behind me.

Oh fuck. Oh no.

I take off after the ball but a Stampede player gets there first, scooping it up and sprinting down the floor. I run at top speed, but my large frame isn't going to beat the wiry defenseman I'm chasing. Wes is gunning for him, too, but is further away than I am. We both watch helplessly as the opposition fakes out our goalie high and then sends a laser of a low shot between his pads.

Game tied, with .5 seconds left on the clock. All the air goes out of the building as the fans process the shock.

We had it. It was right there. All I had to do was catch the fucking ball.

My brain feels fuzzy as I make my way to the bench. My teammates tap me with their sticks to encourage me.

"Keep your head up, Z." Jamie elbows me as I sit down next to him. "Shit happens. I should've made a better pass."

I grumble incoherently, watching the ensuing faceoff and immediate whistle as the officials call for a brief break before overtime begins.

"I'm not thinking about that miss from this point forward, and I hope you aren't either," he asserts. "Let's get back out there and make the next play."

I nod silently, pushing the mistake to the back of my brain as much as possible. Jamie's right. Nothing matters more than the next time we're out on the floor. We can wipe away the missed pass with a goal and win the whole damn thing.

What if this is how the Cinderella magic ends? Because of me?

I shake the self destructive thought out of my head. I'm prone to wallowing, but I've been working to overcome that. The next shift is all that matters.

Overtime starts, and emotions are high on both teams. Sawyer and a Stampede player are jostling each other near the net when Sawyer finally pushes too hard, sending the other player to the ground with a flourish.

"That's a flop!" Coach Travis yells as the ref raises his arm, signaling a penalty. "He's embellishing!"

"Dammit, Sawyer," Jamie mutters under his breath as he walks by on his way to the penalty box.

We head out onto the floor to kill the two minute penalty. My heart is in my throat as we line up for the faceoff. Thankfully we win it handily.

I'm jogging towards the offensive zone when our faceoff specialist gets body checked, the ball popping out of his stick in the process.

Not this again.

I chase down the Stampede player who picks up the ball. I get close enough that he has to slow down and wait for his offense to come onto the floor instead of taking a shot on our net. I'm now stuck on defense, and I'm glad to see Wes and another two defenders come off the bench to back me up.

The Stampede pass back and forth, slowly moving closer to our net. Their star player has the ball, and I put my body in front of him to block his view. I notice his eyes looking past me and towards Wes, who is covering a player near the crease. His stick is lower on his body than it should be while he sizes up the coverage. *That's a mistake.*

I poke the head of his stick with mine, sending the ball flying out towards the midfield line. He looks down in shock, and I take the half second advantage to push past him and thunder after the ball. The other players don't realize what's happening until I'm alone at midfield and running towards their goalie.

Time slows down as I approach, my feet falling heavy on the turf. The crowd noise goes silent in my ears as I read the goaltender's stance for any weak points. I wind up and look at the top right corner of the net. The goalie stays with me until the last second before he commits to the right side. I switch to my backhand and send a shot sailing into the open space above his left shoulder.

The goal horn blares, and it's the best sound I've ever heard.

I howl with elation, smacking my free hand against the glass behind the net where some fans are on their feet screaming. My teammates pile onto me, gloves and sticks accumulating behind us as more and more people throw their equipment off to celebrate. It's overwhelming in the best way possible, and seems to go on forever. Coaches, staff, and media join the fracas as "We Are the Champions" plays throughout the arena.

We did it. We really did it.

Chapter 54

Genny

My heart is about to explode out of my chest. My throat is raw from screaming when Zeke scored a shorthanded goal to win the game. Everyone in the stands is hugging each other and beside themselves with happiness.

I don't realize I'm crying until I push a piece of hair out of my face and feel wetness on my cheek. This is Zeke's dream come true, and I'm out of my mind with joy for him.

The two teams eventually form lines and shake each other's hands, with the Stampede players looking understandably devastated. They had an excellent year, but ran into a team of destiny.

"I always feel so bad for the losing team," my mom says.

"I know, me too," I agree, watching as the Outlaws staff hands out Championship shirts and hats for the players.

"Backwards hats!" Mackenzie hisses, raising her eyebrows at me as the players immediately put the hats on.

"A blessing from the Creator," I say, joining her in respectfully ogling them.

I see Zeke's family and others making their way down to the area where they will enter the playing surface and meet their players. My heart thumps painfully at missing out on the chance to give Zeke a huge hug right now.

"It's my privilege to announce the finals MVP," the league commissioner says from the floor. "Please join me in congratulating Zeke Jacobs of the Buffalo Outlaws."

My jaw drops.

Zeke looks as stunned as I feel, turning and pointing to other players as his teammates push him towards the front. *What an astounding moment for his career.*

Mackenzie puts her arm around me as we watch him shake the Commissioner's hand and accept the MVP trophy. Photographers rush forward to get shots of the moment. A reporter grabs him for an interview, and the audio is broadcast inside the arena.

"Zeke, you've just won a championship and MVP for the first time. What does this moment mean for you?" she asks, holding a microphone in front of him.

Zeke blinks, looking around the arena in awe at the sea of cheering fans. "This means everything to me. It's a dream come true. I'm so grateful to the Creator, who gave us this incredible game of lacrosse that is now shared around the world."

The crowd applauds, and I notice Jamie, Wes, and Sawyer clapping with enthusiasm nearby.

"I also want to take this opportunity to thank my parents." He glances upwards. "My dad, who's not with us anymore, he taught me how to play and to respect the medicine of this game. And my mom, too." He beams and looks over to where Elaine is waiting to come out onto the floor. "She's the strongest person I know."

He pauses, looking nervous.

"Is there anything else you want to share?" the reporter questions with a smile.

"I also want to thank all the Outlaws coaches, staff, and everyone involved with the team, for bringing me here and trusting me to play for this incredible organization." Zeke's eyes scan the arena. "Lastly, I wouldn't be here today if it weren't for my best friend, Genny."

Mackenzie grabs my arm roughly and I freeze.

"She's supported and encouraged me for years, since we were kids, and she's given me a renewed sense of purpose and passion this season," he continues. "Thank you, Gen." His voice softens.

Mackenzie shakes me energetically and my arms swing by my sides.

Orange and white confetti rains down as Jamie, the team captain, is the first to receive the NLL Cup, raising it over his head to the roar of the crowd. He passes it around to the rest of the team, and the crowd cheers as each player and member of staff lifts it in celebration.

"Girl. Go get your man," Mackenzie yells over the noise.

My heart soars. He still loves me. *Of course he does, dummy.* I was afraid to believe it because that would make it harder to keep him away and prevent him breaking my heart again. But being with him is worth the risk of future hurt. I know that deep in my bones.

"Go put that boy out of his misery, Genesee," my mom leans over and shakes my knee, her eyes twinkling.

"Do it for the fans," Mackenzie teases and yanks me to my feet.

The crowd noise and music are deafening. I grip my mom's hand and squeeze myself down our row and into the aisle. Everyone is on their feet cheering and taking pictures, so no one notices me rushing towards the glass on moccasin feet.

No one, that is, except Dusty the opossum.

The Outlaws mascot tries to high five me as I rush by, blocking my path in the process. I attempt to return the gesture but accidentally punch him in his pointy nose instead.

"Oh my gosh, I'm *so sorry*," I cry.

Dusty stumbles back into the handrail, his cowboy hat tumbling to the ground. The fans around us gasp.

"Ma'am, do you need to leave?" A security guard suddenly appears at my elbow.

"No, no. It was just an accident." I retrieve Dusty's headgear and raise onto my tip toes to put it on his head.

The opossum ducks.

I huff. "Well, now you're just being dramatic."

"Is she bothering you, Dusty?" the guard asks.

I fix him with my sternest Auntie glare.

Dusty takes his hat and waves me away.

I glance at security.

"You're free to go, ma'am."

"Thank you!" I take a few steps and spin around. "Is there any chance you could tell me where–"

Dusty jumps behind the guard and peeks at me over his shoulder.

"You know what, never mind."

I have no idea where to go or what to do, so I make my way towards the Zamboni entrance where I'd seen players' families congregating earlier. I hike up my ribbon skirt and climb over the railing dividing it from the seats, much to the horror of the second security guard about to ruin my night.

"Hey! You can't come down here!" He rushes over, standing in front of me once I drop down.

"I'm with the Jacobs family," I explain, a note of desperation creeping into my voice. "Would it be possible to get out onto the floor?"

He shakes his head and blocks me when I take a step to the side. "No, ma'am. Families already went out."

"Please," I plead. "I wasn't sitting with everyone else, so I was late getting here."

"I'm sorry, but no."

Tears prick my eyes as I look out onto the floor, feeling defeated.

By sheer luck, I catch Wes' eye where he's standing nearby with his family. He tilts his head at me for a second, then jogs over and raps loudly on the other side of the glass.

"Hey! Marty!"

The security guard spins his head around in surprise.

"She's with me. She's family." Wes smiles kindly at me.

Marty opens the door with a mumbled apology and I grab Wes' hand in gratitude.

"Thank you so, so much."

"I got you. Come on." He pulls me onto the floor and we wind our way between mobs of players, families, and media. "Zeke is going to be over the fucking moon when he sees you," he yells over the inferno of noise.

My knees are shaking and my heart is pounding. "Sorry, my palms are sweaty," I apologize.

He laughs. "Do you feel mine? I just played a game. I'm disgusting."

He tugs me through a free lane and there's Zeke a few feet in front of me. A backwards ball cap covers his damp hair, and he has a gray championship t-shirt slung over his shoulder. He's grinning from ear to ear, surrounded by his brothers and his mom.

Wes nudges me gently on the back. "Go make his dreams come true."

All the outside noise dulls and I hear my blood rushing in my ears. My mouth feels like cotton, and I'm rooted to the spot I'm standing in. *What if he doesn't want to see me? What if this was a mistake?* The old anxieties come roaring back.

As though he heard me, Zeke looks up. Our eyes meet and my stomach plummets with fear. He blinks, seemingly unsure if he's seeing me correctly. His family follows his gaze, and Elaine's face lights up.

Zeke hands his stick to Jordan and starts walking towards me. I feel sick and dizzy, tempted to spin and run away, but my body remains frozen.

"Gen," he breathes, staring deeply into my eyes, hope vibrating off his broad frame.

Chapter 55

Zeke

It all sits between us: the years of loss and resentment, the joy and electricity of finally being together, the fear of losing a loved one again. In the end, we couldn't trust each other enough to stay and work through being confronted with our demons.

I scan her face, afraid to move and ruin whatever brought her down here. I notice her beaded ears of corn earrings in shades of orange, white, and purple. *Outlaws colors.* It prompts me to turn my gaze lower, and I see she's wearing my jersey t-shirt, but it fits her perfectly so it's not the one from my closet. *Did she just buy that?*

I reach for her hand and bring it to my chest. My heart pounds beneath her palm.

"I can't–" she starts, her voice thick with emotion.

My stomach drops, and my grip tightens on her hand. "Please let me–"

She chokes back a sob, and it breaks my heart wide open.

I don't think, I just sweep her into my arms. She fists my jersey and cries into my shoulder. I wish I could clear everyone out of this building and hold her through the storm.

"*Gönóöhgwa'*," I whisper fiercely against her ear. "I fucked up, and I'm so sorry." I squeeze her tightly. "Words can't express how much I regret the way I reacted to my mom's diagnosis, and how I pushed you away again. I should never have given up on us."

Genny looks up at me with tears glistening in her eyelashes. "I love you, too. I want to love you through this difficult time with your mom." Her hands are shaking and her nails dig into my back.

"I need you. I can't get through this without you," I implore, resting my forehead on hers. My pulse is hammering at her closeness.

"Ditto." She runs her hands up my chest and to my face. "Can we reset the shot clock?"

"We'll call it an over and back."

She nods, grazing her thumb against my bottom lip.

I dip my head and kiss her deeply, bending to lift her feet off the ground and spin her around. She smiles against my lips and wraps her arms around my neck.

Loud whoops of delight break out, and I regretfully tear my mouth away from Genny's to see Wes and Sawyer clapping and high fiving each other. Jamie smiles and nods in my direction.

"You're back!" Sawyer crashes into us and pulls Genny into a rough hug.

She laughs and squeezes him back. "I've missed you guys. Congratulations!"

"You've got to come out with us after this," he insists. "We're taking the Cup on a pub crawl."

I look down at Genny. "Do you want to go?"

She smiles and wraps herself back around me. "Sounds like a good time."

I don't particularly feel like sharing her with my teammates at the moment, but it would be fun to celebrate before getting her all to myself.

We're out celebrating in the confetti with our families for a while before returning to the locker room. Debauchery ensues as players pop open the waiting bottles of champagne and blare music. Sawyer shares his bottle with me and drenches me in fizzy liquid in the process. I laugh and shake out my wet hair like a dog.

"Let's meet up in thirty minutes and take the Cup to a few bars," Sawyer shouts over the music.

"Sounds good."

I gratefully shower off the sweat and alcohol from the previous few hours, get dressed, and head out to find Genny.

Chapter 56

Genny

The Outlaws are drunk, and we're all having a blast.

"Everyone needs to drink out of the Cup!" Sawyer announces, placing it on the bar at Cobblestone. The owners opened the place just for us, since it's a favorite post-game congregation spot for the team.

Neither Zeke or I are big drinkers, but we settle in with some beverages. I don't think he's stopped touching me since he came out of the locker room. He's been holding my hand, draping an arm around me, or resting a hand on my leg the entire time. I'm loving it.

"Hey, lovebirds." Wes plops down at the table where we're sitting, a glass of whiskey in front of him.

We're on a bench seat where Zeke has pulled me into his lap. His arm around my waist holds me to him while he nurses a beer. I had just been about to sneak some kisses down the length of his neck.

"Hey man." Zeke smiles. "How are you feeling?"

Wes grins. "Pretty fucking great. Can't complain about my rookie season."

"You're spoiled now," I tease. "How are you going to top this?"

Wes laughs. "I'll have to think of something. Maybe we go back-to-back next season?"

Zeke raises his glass and clinks it against Wes'. "I'm in if you are."

Wes takes a drink before reaching into his pocket.

"I can't wait to get you home tonight," Zeke's voice rumbles in my ear.

I shiver and turn to him for a kiss. "You want to get out of here soon?"

"Yeah." He wraps both arms around me, pulling me even closer.

I smile contentedly and sneak a peek over at Wes, hoping that our public affection isn't bothering him. He's looking at his phone and wearing the biggest grin.

I tilt my head. "What's up?"

He rubs a hand over his beard, looking decidedly pleased with himself. "Nothing, I just–" He glances back down at his phone before clicking it off and setting it down on the table. "I just heard from someone I didn't expect to."

I raise an eyebrow at him, but I'm distracted by Zeke's hand drifting above my knee and under my skirt.

Jamie joins the table, sitting down with an exhausted sigh and a tall glass of Pepsi.

"Hey Jammer," Wes says with a smile. "You tired?"

Jamie nods and takes a long drink. "I'm too old for this. I was ready for bed as soon as the game was over."

"You're only thirty-four!" I laugh. "You're not old."

"Just wait a few more years until you're thirty," Jamie says. "You'll know exactly what I mean." He shakes around the ice in his cup, trying to reach the final few sips of liquid. "Plus, I want to get home to the kid. He might even still be up after all the festivities."

"You have a kid?" Wes asks in surprise. "How did I not know that?"

Jamie nods. "Yeah, a teenage son. I keep my home life pretty private. Nothing personal, just the way I am."

"Noted." Wes raises his glass of whiskey for a drink.

"We're not far behind you," Zeke says. "We'll be heading out soon, too."

"Mmm hmm," Jamie and Wes hum together, looking at us pointedly.

I blush, and Zeke kisses my cheek.

Sawyer comes crashing over to the table, carrying a precariously balanced tray.

"Shots?" he asks, although it sounds more like a demand.

"That's my cue to peace out," Jamie chuckles. "You all have fun and be safe."

"Yes, Dad!" Sawyer responds cheerfully, distributing a shot glass in front of each of us.

"I shouldn't," Zeke protests. "I need to drive us home."

"Get a hotel room." Sawyer slides into the chair that Jamie just vacated. "The team paid for a block of rooms so players could celebrate tonight."

"For real? That's awesome." I bring the shot glass to my nose and smell its contents. "Is this tequila?"

"Sure is!" Sawyer flags down a waiter, who brings us a bowl full of lime slices.

The three of us groan.

"You are so white, man," Zeke shakes his head.

Tequila is not my drink of choice, but I have to admit the three-step process of salt, shot, and lime is pretty fun to do in a group of friends. My eyes water as I set down my lime slice and fan my face.

"That was brutal," Wes rasps through puckered lips.

"Another round?" Sawyer asks cheerfully, and we all wave our hands in protest.

Chapter 57

Zeke

We eventually peel ourselves away from the party, although it was wrapping up as players ran out of energy and adrenaline. Genny's eyes are getting heavy and I know she's tired.

We claim one of the team rooms at a nearby hotel, and a few others are doing the same. I keep Genny close to me, unwilling to let go of her for fear it's all a dream I'm about to wake up from. I clutch her hand as we leave the check-in desk and head for our room.

We stumble off the elevator with a laugh, feeling tipsy. We find our room number and I fumble with the key card while Genny pulls me to her, her back against the door. My tie has long since come undone and is draped around my neck, which she uses to reel me in.

I moan quietly and kiss her urgently while she unbuttons the top of my dress shirt.

"Hey you two! Get a room!" Sawyer catcalls, walking past us in the hallway with a grin.

I flip him off and finally get a hold of the key card in my pocket, holding it against the scanner and opening the door. I grip Genny around the waist to prevent her from falling backwards into the room.

Every few feet, we shed articles of clothing until we reach the bed, desperate for each other. She has always enjoyed getting me out of my suit after games. This time, however, her fingers are messy but determined as opposed to leisurely. I pull her shirt over her head and carefully slide her ribbon skirt down her legs.

"This is beautiful," I say. "Did you make this?"

"I did," she replies breathily, unbuckling my belt. "Yesterday."

I bite back a groan as she fumbles with the buttons on my pants. "Yesterday?"

Genny frowns and continues trying to reach the inside button along my waistband. "Yes. This was a bit of a last-minute decision."

"Would you like some help?" I smile down at her, amused at her frustration.

"No," she huffs.

I give her another few seconds but can't wait any longer. I pick her up and wrap her legs around my waist, lowering her onto the bed a bit harder than I'd intended.

"Hey!" she complains while I sit back to finish unbuttoning my slacks.

Her annoyance turns to desire as she watches me undress.

"Oh, Zeke," she breathes when I settle between her legs. "I've missed you so much."

I run a hand up her back and unhook her bra, tossing it off the bed. "There's no possible way you've missed me as much as I've missed you."

She opens her mouth to protest and I silence her with a kiss. I want to consume her. My hands are everywhere.

She wraps her legs around my waist, pulling me against her as she writhes against my hardness. "I need you."

I grip her thighs, feeling my self control slipping. "Not yet. I want to take my time with you."

She squeezes my hips tighter. "You can get me off all night if you want. Just please get inside me now."

I groan and untangle her legs from around me so I can pull her panties aside. "Promise? Because I will keep you up until sunrise if you let me."

"I promise."

Genny takes in a quick breath as I enter her. She feels *so damn good.* I'm holding myself so taut in order to slow down and not hurt her. She moans and wraps her legs back around me, pulling me in deeper. *Fuck.*

She winds her arms around my neck, drawing my mouth down to hers. I lower to my forearms, our bodies melding together as I press into her.

It's rough and needy, and we're both gasping for breath when I eventually collapse next to her. I pull her into my arms and my heart rate begins to slow.

"I love you so much," I murmur, nipping at her earlobe.

She hums in appreciation. "I love you, too." Her tousled hair has come undone and spreads onto my biceps.

I hold her for a few minutes before raising up on my elbow. "What do you mean this was a last-minute decision?"

Genny looks up at me. "Huh?"

"You said you made your ribbon skirt yesterday, because it was a last-minute decision to come to the game."

She bites her lip, looking sheepish. "Well, yes. It was."

"What made you come by my place on Wednesday?" I ask, dying to know how her change of heart came about.

She sighs, tracing circles along that tattoo on my chest. "I read your letters."

I come up to my forearm. "You did? I figured you smudged all traces of me out of your house," I tease.

"I would've, but Mackenzie came to your defense," she smiles.

"Ah, a lucky break." I kiss the top of her head. "Thank you for reading them. It's been really therapeutic to write them, even knowing you might never see them."

She snuggles into me and runs her thumb along my jawline. "I'm so proud of you, Zeke," she says quietly, her eyes bright. "I know how hard it must've been for you to ask for help and re-examine all this old stuff again."

I smile and kiss her palm. "It was, but I also knew it was the only way through the shitstorm I'd gotten myself into. I needed to be better for my family. For my team. For you." I lace my fingers through hers. "Even if you never forgave me, I couldn't let you believe you were at fault. At all. I needed you to know how adored you are."

She pulls me to her for a soft kiss full of emotion.

"And how very beautiful you are," I continue against her lips. "You're so goddamn sexy."

She giggles. "You didn't say anything like that in your letters."

"Well, no. You definitely would've burned them if I had." I gently roll Genny onto her back, my attention turning to her breasts.

"I love you," she moans as I take one of her nipples into my mouth.

"Do I really get to have you all night?" I ask, kissing between her breasts and down her ribcage.

She chuckles with a groan. "I may come to regret that negotiation tactic."

"We'll see about that." I flip her again, this time onto her stomach. My fingers slide into her from behind and she moans so loudly she grabs for a pillow. "Why don't you keep track of how many times I can make you finish before the sun comes up?"

She squirms but I hold her in place, loving how her protests immediately transform into needy sighs. I've got all the energy in the world for her.

By the time dawn has started to paint the sky, I have an exhausted and thoroughly satisfied Genny in my arms.

"Do I need to have you back in time for school?" I ask, kissing her hair.

"It's Memorial Day," she mumbles, her voice fading from fatigue. "I have the day off."

I clasp her more tightly to me. "I forgot about that. Then let's rest."

I look down, and she's already asleep. I pull the blankets up around her shoulders with a smile, keeping her on my chest.

In the past twelve hours, the Outlaws won the NLL Cup, I was awarded MVP of the championship series, and Genny had come back to me. We'd made love all night, and now she was asleep in my arms for the next few hours.

Best day ever.

I tuck her under my chin and begin to doze off, the happiest man in the world.

Epilogue

One month later

Genny

I hear the early summer rain pinging off the roof as I drift back into consciousness. A cool breeze blows gently through the open window next to the bed, and I burrow deeper under my blanket. I'm on the verge of falling back asleep when a soft clunk on the nightstand pulls me awake.

"Sorry. I wasn't trying to wake you." Zeke looks down apologetically, his hand still wrapped around the steaming mug of coffee he'd set next to me.

"It's OK. Getting coffee in bed with you is much better than sleeping, anyway," I smile, reaching for the pocket of his black sweatpants so I can pull him to me.

He sets his own mug down and sits on the edge of the bed. He leans over to give me a soft kiss, and I pull more determinedly on his waistband. He chuckles against my lips and lays next to me, wrapping me in his arms as I scoot back to make room for him.

"I could get used to this," I sigh against his chest, my eyes closing happily.

"You might need to," he teases, brushing some hair out of my face. "I've got ten years of coffee and breakfast in bed to make up for."

I lightly skate my nails down the delicious grooves in his chest and stomach before drifting past his waistband. "I can think of some other things we have to make up for." I gently wrap my hand around him and squeeze, eliciting a quiet groan.

Zeke's hand comes up to frame my face as he pulls me closer to him. His kiss still lights me on fire as much as the first one, and I shudder as his breath skates over me before he lowers his mouth to mine.

"As much as I want to follow that line of thinking, we need to head up to Buffalo soon," he laments.

"Oh, that's right!" My sleepy brain had forgotten what day it was.

It's Elaine's last day of treatment at the cancer hospital. Her infusions had been touch and go at the start, but the end result was an overwhelming success. She has yet to be declared officially cancer-free, but her labs have been showing dramatic improvement, and the doctors have decided today is the last infusion she'll need for now.

The Jacobs family is bringing me along to her final treatment. She'll get to ring the bell at the hospital afterwards, a symbolic act of hope and resilience against cancer. It's been a long and scary road, but as of today the future is bright.

"I suppose you're right." I bite my lip and trace my finger down the length of him. "We can wait until later."

"Well, if we're quick about it..." Zeke's voice trails off as he pushes me down into the mattress, and I giggle against his lips.

Later, the six of us pile into Jordan's car, stopping along the way to pick up Delores. The mood is jovial as we approach the culmination of such a hard stretch of months. Ezra graduated from SUNY Geneseo last month, I'm on summer break, and Zeke is on a bye week from his field lacrosse team. Jordan and Miles' fledgling construction business is picking up with summer projects. Life feels good right now.

Zeke accompanies his mom into the treatment room for a few hours while his family and I catch up and chat. It's been nearly a month since the Outlaws' championship win, and I've been finishing up my school year while spending extra time with Zeke. The warmth and extra daylight of summer have lifted all our spirits.

We gather around the bell with hospital staff to greet Elaine once her session is complete. Her eyes are shiny with tears as she wraps an arm around Zeke's waist to steady herself.

"Thank you all for being here," she says emotionally. "I know how difficult this has been on all of us, not just me."

I bite my cheek to keep my tears at bay.

"I needed every one of you to get through this, and I'm so grateful for all of your love, support, and time these past four months." She reaches for my hand and squeezes it with a smile. "My family is incredible."

"They learn from the best," a nurse says, and Elaine beams.

She rings the bell and we all cheer. We know better than to assume that the cancer is gone forever, but for now we can celebrate and let our guards down a little bit.

We go out for lunch in Buffalo to observe the occasion before heading home, all of us full and stuffed into the SUV together. There's nowhere else I'd rather be.

Zeke and I lay on the couch together afterwards. He traces up and down my bare arms as we watch a movie. My eyes are heavy as I start to doze on his chest.

"Gen?"

I can barely keep my eyes open. "Yeah?"

"Can we do this forever?"

I look up at him. "Do what?"

He leans down to kiss my forehead. "This. Just being together."

"We'll have to go to work, eventually."

He chuckles. "Besides that." He folds his arms around my upper body. "I'd like to keep you for a long, long time."

My stomach flutters. "I'd like that, too."

"You're not going to be able to get rid of me this time."

"Well, thank Creator for that."

Acknowledgements

Niawen'kó:wa to the Haudenosaunee community across Turtle Island for the welcome I have always received as a *Kanien'kehá:ka* woman who grew up off-reserve. There's always more to learn, and it is a joy to do so.

This book would not be possible without the All Write Well community, and Maria Secoy most of all. Thank you for believing in me and providing endless support as I felt my way along the unfamiliar landscape of publishing.

Thank you to my friends and beta readers: Reannen, Carole, Connie, and Kirby. This book grew so much under your thoughtful feedback and encouragement.

I am deeply grateful for my husband, Brad, who steered our family's ship while I spent every free moment writing and realizing my lifelong dream of publishing a novel. He is my North Star and lacrosse vibes checker.

Growing up as an urban Native of mixed ancestry, the opportunity was there for my parents to disregard our Mohawk traditions. Instead, they fought for them. *Konnorónhkwa*.

I consulted a number of authentic voices in my research:

Akhwatsirehkó:wa: My Big Family by Brennor Jacobs with Brendan Bomberry

Seneca Nation of Indians Official Website (https://sni.org)
Seneca Dictionary (https://seneca-dictionary.com)

About the author

S.E. Martin is an enrolled member of the Mohawk Nation at Six Nations of the Grand River reserve in Ohsweken, Ontario. She grew up in Niagara Falls, NY and currently resides in New England with her husband and children. She's been writing personally and professionally since her teenage years. She has always been captivated by the power of a good story. She's writing The Medicine Game series in order to share the beauty of Haudenosaunee culture and the game of lacrosse with a wider audience. When she's not reading or writing, you can find her losing years off her lifespan by cheering for Buffalo sports teams. *Over and Back* is her debut novel.

Connect With Me

The Medicine Game Series

- **Over and Back:** A childhood friends-to-lovers, second chance romance on the Seneca Nation

- **Hidden Ball Trick:** A friends with benefits, secret dating romance featuring the Oneida Nation

- **Trick Shot**: A frenemies-to-lovers, second chance romance involving the Tuscarora Nation